TURNING ON A DIME

a time-travel adventure

Also by Maggie Dana

TURNING
ON A
DIME

Maggie Dana

For Ron
best wishes
Maggie Dana

PP
PAGEWORKS PRESS

ISBN 978-0-9851504-9-5

Edited by Judith Cardanha
Cover by Margaret Sunter
Interior design by Anne Honeywood
Published by Pageworks Press
Text set in Sabon

To Paul who always listened, then told me I could.

1

SAMANTHA

Connecticut, present day

NUGGET FLICKS HIS EARS as we trot down the center-line. Our approach is crooked and I can see Dad watching us, frowning beneath the brim of his faded Red Sox cap. It's been a bad ride—two botched half passes, three rough transitions, and an extended trot that felt more like harness racing than a dressage test.

Sweat trickles slowly down my neck. It creeps between my shoulder blades and lays its sticky fingers on my spine.

I'd give anything to wipe my face, but I can't because that's not what you do, even when you're only practicing. You're supposed to smile and pretend to be having a great time, never mind that your legs are now shattered and want to disown you.

"Samantha, don't sit there like a potted plant," Dad hollers. *"Hielen omlaag."*

That's Dutch for *"Heels down."*

My father is third-generation American but his family is from Holland and he's taught me enough Dutch to get along when we go over there.

"And, Samantha," Dad says, just to rub it in, "ballet lessons are on Tuesdays."

I guess he didn't like my pirouette at the canter that probably looked as if I were torturing poor Nugget. "Not your fault," I whisper, patting his sweaty shoulder.

Nugget is not your typical dressage horse. He's not a rich, dark brown or an elegant bay with white socks and a perfect star. He's a flashy chestnut gelding with a blond mane and tail that my mother says would put Farrah Fawcett to shame.

"Who's she?" I'd asked over dinner.

Mom and Dad had exchanged glances. My brother Erik had laughed and slapped his thighs. "Hot babe."

"Charlie's Angels," Mom said.

"Huh?"

"Before your time," Erik said.

He's nineteen, only four years older than I am, but sometimes he turns those four years into a generation. He likes the old movies and TV shows that my parents like. I couldn't care less about any of them. If it's got a horse in it, I'll watch it; otherwise—

My phone rings.

Dad hates it when I interrupt our lessons to take a call, but it might be Jenna, so—

"We won!" she yells.

Dad's explanation about flying changes goes in one ear and out the other. "What?" I yell back.

"The beach lottery, you idiot."

"You're kidding." It's not easy, listening to Dad while Jenna's shouting at me.

But, wow . . . the beach lottery?

It's a huge deal around here—well, for horse people it is. The winners get to ride on a private beach in midsummer which means we'll be riding bareback in bathing suits, jumping waves, and swimming with our horses. This is not something you can do at our town beach.

The lifeguards would have a meltdown.

They go ballistic if you walk a dog on the sand, never mind ride a horse. You can only do it in winter when it's freezing cold and you're bundled up like an Eskimo.

"Earth to Sam," Jenna intones. "This is *not* a joke."

"When?"

"Sunday," she says.

My heart sinks. "I can't."

"Yes, you *can*," says my father. "You just need more leg on the girth and Nugget will—"

Trouble is, he's not talking about the beach lottery, which I never thought Jenna and I had a chance of winning. But I can't let Dad down. We're flying to Mississippi this weekend to look at horses and I'll be riding them for him.

My father doesn't ride any more.

Two years before I was born he was shortlisted for the Olympics. But a freak accident put him out of action when his horse crashed into a double oxer, trapping Dad beneath it and shattering his left knee into a dozen tiny pieces.

His Olympic dream now burns inside me.

Samantha DeVries—rhymes with freeze—the first African American to ride in the Olympic Games.

"Sam," Jenna says, "wake up."

Dad's still talking—something about half-halts and my outside rein—but I'm not paying attention, even though I desperately need to. If I want to realize my dream—and his—I have to work harder.

My father's name, Lucas DeVries, opens many doors in the horse world, but as he keeps reminding me, I need to be good enough to actually ride through those doors.

"I'm here," I say.

"Not *this* Sunday," Jenna says, laughing. "Our beach ride is *next* Sunday." There's a pause. "After you get back, okay?"

"*Okay*," I say.

Undeterred, my father nods. "I'm so glad you understand," he says. "Now let's get on with this lesson, and then you need to work on your judo."

Dad's teaching me that as well.

He says it helps with balance and coordination. It also helps with the bullies at school. They've learned not to mess with me any more.

Mom leans against the doorframe while I pack. She's the guardian angel of teenage travelers. If she weren't here prodding me, I'd wind up in Mississippi with ten pairs of woolly socks, no bras, and a ratty old toothbrush I scrubbed Nugget's bit with.

"You need a trim," she says.

I run a hand through my thick hair. It hangs below my shoulders, and trying to squash it all into a bun so I can cram my riding helmet on without giving myself a headache is a major challenge.

"Next week," I say, pawing through piles of laundry for clean t-shirts and breeches that don't have holes in them. Mom looks around my room. She sighs, and I know what's coming next.

"Isn't this all a bit . . . much?"

And I grin, because of course it is.

My bedroom is exactly what every horse-crazy girl wants—wall-to-wall posters of show jumpers, ribbons strung about like bunting, and photos of every pony you've ever ridden pinned all over your bulletin board. Oh, and let's not forget the Breyer models, the shelves full of dog-eared favorites like *Black Beauty* and *My Friend Flicka*, and that wooden rocking horse you can't bear to get rid of because you still ride it when nobody's looking.

Flopping onto my bed, I wrap myself in the pony-print comforter Mom bought me when I was ten. No way will I give all this up—even when I get married, which my brother says will never happen because whoever marries me would have to marry my horse as well.

Yeah, right.

The cute guy I'm crushing on rides a snowboard, not a horse. Plus, he's a senior and I'm a sophomore. He has no clue I exist because he's on another planet with razzle-dazzle snowboards and snow bunny cheerleaders dressed like Icicle Barbie.

"How did your lesson go?" Mom says, twisting the pearl ring she always wears—even at the beach.

The beach?

"Guess what?" I say. "We won."

"The beach lottery?"

"Yeah."

"Awesome." Mom gives me a high five like I knew she would, then she does a happy dance around my room. This is what I love about my mom. She totally gets being a teenager. "When is it?"

"Sunday."

"But you won't be able to go."

"*Next* Sunday," I say. "After we get home."

"Which reminds me. You'd better pack a dress."

I sit up. "What?"

"You know," my mother says, rolling her eyes the way I do. "A garment that doesn't require you to stick both legs into it separately."

Hangers rattle as Mom rummages through my closet and pulls out a lime green dress with puffy sleeves I vaguely remember wearing in eighth grade. She holds it up and we both shake our heads.

"Okay, so how about this?"

That's better. A jeans skirt I can handle.

"With proper shoes," she adds. "Not paddock boots or sneakers, okay?" From beneath my dresser she pulls out a pair of dusty espadrilles.

I can handle those, too.

After Mom leaves, I shove the important stuff into my knapsack—iPhone, earbuds, and a photocopy of Nugget's pedigree. I'm taking it with me because some of my horse's ancestors were bred in Mississippi and I'm hoping to find out more about them.

There are more than fifteen generations on the pedigree. I've memorized the recent ones, but not those further down the list. Most say *grade mare* or *unknown* which doesn't give me a lot to go on.

Mom's the one who got me started on this. She's digging into her own past and spends hours online with genealogy databases trying to find out more about her history. Right now, she's stuck at 1875; and no matter what lead she follows, she can't seem to get any further back.

I hope I have better luck.

Most of our horses are sleeping when I slip into the barn. The younger ones are lying down, eyes closed and totally relaxed, but the older ones sleep standing up.

Nugget is wide awake.

He whickers as I open his stall door, then nudges my pockets for a treat.

"You are *so* spoiled I say," feeding him apple chunks and carrots. He slobbers juice down my t-shirt. "Be good for Jenna, okay?"

She's coming over to help Mom with the horses while Dad and I are gone. We'll be home on Monday—three days from now—and already it feels like a lifetime away. I guess it's because we're going to a place I've never been before.

2

CAROLINE

Mississippi, July 1863

THE MINUTE MY PARENTS' CARRIAGE leaves our driveway, I bolt from my room and race down the stairs. With luck, I'll be able to slip outside without being seen. But I have to be careful. Mama's spies—the housekeeper, the cook, and the upstairs maid—are everywhere and they know I've been forbidden to go to the barn.

No horses, no riding for a week.

My punishment is supposed to end tomorrow, but last night, Mama dropped a cannon ball. I'm to spend the next five days visiting friends—hers, not mine—and they're sending a carriage to pick me up later this afternoon. If I don't risk seeing Pandora now, I won't get to see her till next Thursday.

Gathering up my cotton skirts, I leap down the last three steps and land on the foyer's wet marble floor. Mops, brushes,

and soapy water go flying as I slide in a most unladylike fashion into Mama's favorite bombé chest.

"Ouch."

I'd say a lot more—like the words I've learned from my
brother—but there's a slave girl cowering in the corner. She
looks at me, eyes wide with fright as if expecting to be beaten.

"You're new here, aren't you?" Struggling to my feet, I
rub my sore elbows and want to rub the bits of me that really
hurt, but don't dare because the girl is watching.

She nods, tense as a coiled spring.

In her slender brown hands, she holds a small book. It
looks like a diary of some sort. But slaves can't read or write
because nobody teaches them; it's not allowed. So what is this
girl doing with a book?

"Give it to me," I say.

Reluctantly, she hands it over. Its yellowing pages are covered with lines of neat writing, and it reminds me of my lessons with Alice Hamilton whose precise penmanship caused
Mama to reach for her smelling salts. After she recovered her
equilibrium, Mama dismissed our tutor and found another,
but it didn't do any good. My handwriting is still illegible.

"Is the book yours?" I say.

The girl makes a choking sound. She can't be any more
than fifteen, the same age as me.

"What's your name?" I say.

"Pearl."

"The housekeeper will be angry if she catches you with
this," I say, closing the book and giving it to her. "You'd
better hide it, and then you'd better clean up this mess."

"Yes, ma'am," she says.

Her big brown eyes are like the pansies in my mother's garden. For a moment she stares at me as if we're equals—just a couple of girls who've been caught breaking the rules.

None of the other slaves do this. They always look down and shuffle off. Feeling an odd sense of guilt that I can't explain, I limp into the dining room and scoop two rosy red apples from a bowl on the table.

Another sin.

"I'll keep quiet about your book," I say, hiding the apples beneath my shirt, "if you promise not to tell you saw me."

"Are those for the horses?"

Her voice is barely above a whisper, yet it sounds loud enough to draw Mama's maid from the parlor. If she catches me here, I'll be in more trouble than I already am.

I catch my breath. "Yes."

With a secret little smile, the slave girl nods and picks up a mop.

My bootlaces snap like buggy whips as I race into the barn. I stop to retie my leather bows and a lock of hair falls loose from my messy braid.

Mama calls it "honey brown."

It's not. It's just plain old brown, but Mama likes to dress things up with fancy words. She says my sister's hair is like spun gold, and she's always making Louise rinse it in lemon juice to turn it even lighter. There are times I want to drink my sister's hair, especially on hot days like this one.

Horses—black, brown, and chestnut—stick their heads

over stall doors as I run down the barn's wide center aisle. But I can't resist Papa's gorgeous horses, so I stop to pat noses and stroke forelocks.

These are the famous Chandler horses that my father's family has been breeding for almost fifty years. Some are munching hay; others have flecks of grain on their whiskers. Unlike me, they've already had breakfast. I pull out an apple and sink my teeth into it. Juice dribbles down my chin as I approach the last stall—Pandora's.

For a moment I stop and just look at her.

She's the most gorgeous horse in the world—a bright bay with wide-set eyes, a black tail that almost reaches the ground, and a perfect little star in the center of her forehead. She whickers hopefully, so I feed her the rest of my apple.

"Pandora," I say, "I've missed you."

She tries to whicker again, but slobbers juice down my shirt instead, adding to the mess I've already made. I move her silky black forelock to one side and plant a kiss on her star.

"I wanted to come and see you," I say, opening her stall door, "but Mama wouldn't let me out of the house."

Pandora gives a little nod as if she knows all about it. Well, she does, because last Friday I rode her bareback into the duck pond. She loved it and so did I, but the stupid ducks ruined everything. They quacked loud enough to spook Pandora and wake Mama from her nap. She looked out the window in time to see me sail off Pandora's back and land in two feet of muddy water. I was confined to the house for a week and forbidden, yet again, to ride bareback.

"But, Mama," I wailed, "would you rather I ruin my saddle?"

"No, I'd rather you didn't embarrass this family by riding like a farm boy," my mother said. "You're fifteen years old, Caroline Chandler. It's time you started acting like a young lady."

I wrap my arms around Pandora's well-muscled neck.

Oh, dear.

I'm not supposed to think about muscles. That's what boys have—and horses—but girls aren't allowed to notice or even learn about them.

Fortunately my father has books on equine anatomy in his library and I've borrowed quite a few. The last time I was in there I picked up one of Papa's science magazines because it had a horse on the cover. Flicking through it I found a short story about a man who traveled into the future. They had flying machines and horseless carriages and tall buildings that reached to the sky. It's amazing what you can learn from a book.

Quite shocking, really.

Mama would lock me up forever if she found out what I'd been reading. Some of it makes me blush redder than the apples I stole from the dining room table, especially the part about foals being born.

I think Papa knows, though.

But he hasn't said anything. He just gives me knowing smiles and sometimes asks questions that I'm not supposed to know the answers to, but I do.

"Mama even made me practice the piano," I whisper into Pandora's black mane. "Then she insisted I try on that horrible pink dress. It's got dozens of buttons and too many ruffles, and when she laced me into that awful corset, I couldn't breathe."

Louise, my older sister, is getting married in September and I'm to be one of the bridesmaids. The thought of wearing long gloves and a hat with ribbons and flowers appalls me. Hoping for sisterly sympathy, I'd turned to Louise but discovered that she was mad at me too.

Pandora nuzzles my hand, so I give her the other apple. Nobody else rides her because she won't let them. When Papa first figured this out he tried to sell Pandora but couldn't find a buyer. Not even the Confederate Army was willing to take a chance on a mare that threw everyone, except me, off her back.

It was the trainer's fault.

After I'd done all the basics with Pandora—ground driving and long-lining—she showed such promise that Papa sent her to a professional trainer who, we found out later, used sticks instead of carrots. So Pandora attacked him and got sent home in disgrace. After that, she never allowed another man on her back, not even my brother, Theo, who's as gentle with horses as I am.

"I'll come back in a minute," I tell her, giving her sweet nose another kiss. "And we'll go for a ride. But first, I have to change my clothes."

Hitching up my skirts, I look at my bare legs.

No pantalettes, no petticoats, either. Just this horrible skirt that I'll get rid of as soon as I retrieve my brother's old breeches that I've hidden in the hayloft.

A clump of hay lands at my feet.

I look up.

Another explodes all over my face.

"Theo Chandler, I'll get you for this," I say, spitting out seeds and bits of hay. "What are you doing up there?"

"Waiting," says my brother.

3

SAMANTHA

Connecticut, present day

MY BROTHER DRIVES Dad and me to the airport. As usual, Erik's plugged into his iPod, listening to an audiobook. One of his favorites is *The Time Machine* and he's raved about it so much that I could probably write a book report on it and totally dazzle my English teacher.

In front of the terminal, Erik snags a parking spot meant for taxis and lets Dad and me out. We grab our luggage and my brother takes off wicked fast because there's a line of angry drivers behind him, honking like mad.

"Phew," Dad says, wiping his brow.

It's even hotter than it was yesterday. I hope Nugget's inside with the barn's fans going at full blast. Will the barn in Mississippi have fans? Probably not. I bet their barns are air conditioned. Once again, I check my knapsack. I have Nugget's papers, my cell phone, and its charger. There's a text from Jenna.

miss you. so does copper.

Copper—short for Copernicus—is Jenna's chestnut gelding. He looks so much like Nugget, it's kind of freaky. When we compete in shows together, people get our horses muddled up.

But they don't get Jenna and me muddled up.

I'm what my hip generation calls a *halfie*, a mixed-race kid, and Jenna loves to push my buttons by saying I'm the color that white folks try to be when they go to Florida and lie in the sun for two months.

We fall over laughing about this.

Some people think I'm Hawaiian, which isn't a stretch given my family's hodgepodge of ancestors. I wouldn't be surprised if King Kamehameha was in there somewhere mixed up with Dad's Dutch royalty.

Yes, royalty.

My grandfather's second cousin was a Dutch count or whatever they're called. But that's okay because the Dutch royal family is kind of cool. They don't talk with plums in their mouths and pretend they're better than anyone else like other royals do. Dad says Queen Juliana used to ride her bicycle on the streets of Amsterdam—no bodyguards or helmet either, unless you counted her hair which looked as if it had been squirted on with a glue gun.

I think she probably rode horses, too.

Sadly, Dad and I don't move like Dutch royalty through

the airport's check-in procedure. There are no palace flunkies with obsequious smiles and willing hands to guide us past the lines of people waiting to have their belongings, and their feet, scanned for contraband. Jenna texts again.

r u stuck?

yes

bummer. how long?

like, 4-ever

It reminds me of waiting our turn to ride. At shows, we'd circle the warm-up ring, keeping an eye on each other, and then worry like crazy when either of us was in the arena. If Jenna got a ribbon, I was ecstatic. When I won, Jenna would pump the air with her fist and together we'd ride around the show grounds like two puppies let loose from a cage.

Dad and I shuffle forward in line.

We pass inspection despite the metal pins in Dad's bum knee setting off all the alarms, and end up slouched in uncomfortable chairs while waiting for our flight. According to my fuzzy math it takes less time to fly from Connecticut to Mississippi than it does to drive fifty miles from our house to the airport and hang about in endless lines. But that's the way it is these days.

Hurry up and wait.

4

CAROLINE

Mississippi, July 1863

"WHO ARE YOU waiting for?" I call to my brother.

"You."

"Why?"

"Because I need someone to talk to," he says.

More hay flutters down. "How did you know where to find me?"

Theo peers at me through the hayloft's opening. "Where else would you be the moment Mama's back is turned?"

My brother has almond-shaped green eyes, just like me, but his are fringed with pale lashes. From a distance, it looks as if he doesn't have any eyelashes at all. Mine are long, dark, and curly.

"Spider-leg lashes," Theo always teases.

It makes me shudder.

To keep from stepping on my skirt, I stuff the hem between my teeth and use both hands to climb the ladder that leads into the hayloft. It's more familiar than my bedroom.

When Theo and I were younger we used to hide beneath piles of sweet-smelling hay and spy through cracks in the floorboards on the grownups below, listening to them discuss horse pedigrees and whose stallion had sired the most winners. Sometimes Theo made me cover my ears. I never let on that I knew exactly what they were talking about, thanks to the books I'd borrowed from Papa's library.

"I'll listen," I say, "but only if you promise not to tell Mama I was in the barn."

Theo sighs, like he always does, then turns away to give me a little privacy while I step out of my skirt and pull on the old breeches that Theo has outgrown. I tuck in the white muslin shirt—something else I've borrowed from my brother.

At sixteen, he's not old enough to join the Confederate army, but I'm still worried. The war between the states has been raging for two years and I've heard stories of boys his age—and even younger—being wounded and getting killed.

He says, "Did you hear what happened at Vicksburg?"

"Papa told me and Louise about it last night."

"What did he say?"

"Not much." I shrug because the war doesn't interest me. "Papa said there's been a big battle and the North has won, but that we'll win the next one."

"It was a siege," Theo says. "General Grant's troops surrounded the city. His gunboats shelled Vicksburg from the river. People abandoned their homes and hid in caves. No food or supplies got through." He pauses and looks at me. "Our soldiers surrendered because they were starving."

I shudder and wish I had another apple to bite into. But I don't, because Pandora ate it. I try to imagine being hungry and I can't. Despite the war, food is still plentiful at our plantation.

"Papa says those murdering Yankees won't bother with us," I say. "There's nothing for them here."

Theo hesitates. "Oh, but there is."

"Like what?"

"Fresh horses."

A horrified silence stretches between us. "Papa would never allow it," I finally say.

"If the soldiers want horses, they'll take them," Theo replies.

"*Our* soldiers?"

He nods. "The Yankees as well. They've been stealing horses and looting homes all through the South."

I try to understand, but it doesn't make any sense. Why would people who speak the same language and share the same country go to war?

"Papa says the North doesn't believe we should own slaves," I say, thinking about Pearl and the way she'd looked at me, as bold as a young horse. "But our slaves are happy; they don't run off."

"Your maid did," Theo says.

I'm still smarting over that. People will think I abused her but I didn't. I wanted to give Ruth my old dresses, but Mama didn't approve, so I'd sneak sugary treats into my room after supper and share them with Ruth. She and I played together when we were little, before we both grew up and everything changed.

Yesterday, I overheard Beulah, my mother's maid, telling the cook that Ruth had run off to join something called the Underground Railroad. I've heard whispers about this. It helps slaves get to the North and freedom.

I cross my fingers for Ruth.

If she gets caught by our overseer, she'll get a whipping, so I'm hoping she's far away by now. I just wish she'd said good-bye. I wouldn't have told anyone about her plans. I really wouldn't.

"We treat our people well," I say, then take a long look at my brother. "Is that so terribly wrong?"

"No, it's not," he says. "But slavery is. According to our country's Constitution, all men are created equal."

"Papa doesn't think so."

"I know," Theo says. "And neither do the other slave owners."

"What about you?" I say. "What do you think?"

He takes a deep breath. "The more I hear about the war, the less convinced I am that we're right."

"Have you told Papa how you feel?"

Theo looks at me as if I'm mad. "Of course not."

This sounds like heresy, a contradiction of everything we've been brought up to believe. "But we can't manage without slaves," I say.

"We can if we try."

"Don't be foolish," I say. "We need the Negroes to pick our cotton and clean our houses. Who else is going to do it?"

"Ah," Theo says. "That's the big question."

His words stir up all sorts of ambivalent feelings I've been trying to quell. Slavery confuses me, but animals don't. They're a whole lot less complicated. "So, what do we do about our horses?" I ask.

"Hide them."

"How?"

"That's just it," Theo says. "I don't know."

I sit down to retie my boots. Theo has raised more questions than he's answered. This really isn't going to affect us, is it? The war couldn't be this close. Theo has to be all wrong.

"You're overreacting," I say, scrambling to my feet. "Papa wouldn't allow his horses to be taken away."

Theo sighs. "Let's hope it doesn't come to that."

5

SAMANTHA

Mississippi, present day

IT'S A ROUGH FLIGHT from Connecticut to Mississippi
—even worse than yesterday's dressage lesson, but with tornadoes. Out the plane's window I see a wall of gray cloud so
I pull down the blind. Dad tries to distract me with stories
about his old college roommate, the guy we're going to stay
with.

"Hugh's a Civil War buff," Dad says.

"And a horse breeder."

"That, too," my father says. "He told me that more
horses than soldiers were killed in the Civil War."

"It's wrong to drag animals into a war," I say, shuddering.
"They didn't start it, so why—?"

Just then, the plane hits an air pocket and sinks like a
stone.

Dad squeezes my hand. "Not long now."

"If we make it."

But we do, and we're the last flight to land.

All the others have been diverted. So, it seems, has our rental car. Dad has to make a dozen phone calls to get us a last-minute rent-a-wreck with more bumper stickers than a hippie's van.

We head west toward Vicksburg, site of yet another Civil War battle that my mother's been trying to get me interested in. History is her passion; sadly, it's not mine except when it comes to Nugget's family tree.

Dad says I'm chasing rainbows.

An hour later we drive past a sign for *Heritage Meadows*. They breed Dutch Warmbloods, same as my father does, but their horses also have a trace of other breeds mixed in which is why I'm interested. This might not be the same farm where Nugget's ancestors came from, but it's a good place to start. Plus they've got a daughter my age, so maybe I'll have someone to hang out with this weekend.

Dad pulls into a long gravel driveway bordered on both sides by paddocks filled with horses—bays, browns, and chestnuts—grazing peacefully amid lush grass that I didn't expect to see this far south. I guess they've had more rain than we've had. In a smaller paddock, a magnificent black horse struts the fence line. He raises his head and lets out a challenging neigh.

The barn's stallion, I'm guessing.

The paddocks give way to a tunnel of enormous trees that arch over the driveway like something from a Tolkien book. Creepy and gorgeous, all at once.

"Live oak," my father says.

I grin. "As opposed to dead ones?"

He tells me that the feathery gray stuff hanging from them is called Spanish moss. "It's an air plant," Dad says, then slows down so I can take a photo.

Ahead is a white plantation house, so perfect and so elegant it's as if we've strayed onto the set of a car commercial. At any moment, a sleek black Mercedes or a Jaguar will glide beneath the porte cochère—fancy name for a front porch with fluted columns—and disgorge a beautiful couple in evening dress. An English butler wearing a tailcoat and starched collar will dispense glasses of champagne from a silver tray, and—

"We're here," Dad says.

Our car skids to a halt so fast my head snaps forward and I almost get whiplash.

"Welcome," booms a loud voice.

Not exactly the butler, but still . . .

There's a flurry of introductions. Dad slaps this silver-haired guy on the back and they exchange a weird college handshake—thumbs sticking up, fingers splayed—while grinning at each other like a pair of goofy teenagers. Dad had told me they hadn't seen one another in more than twenty years.

That would be around the time that my father divorced Erik's mother for running off and leaving him with a six-month-old baby—my brother. Two years later, Dad married Mom, so I'm real happy about that, otherwise I wouldn't even be here.

Dad says, "Hughie-Dewey."

"Luke the Duke," says the guy.

Behind him is a woman with lips drawn so tight it's obvious she doesn't approve of old college nicknames. Her skin is so pale she's almost transparent. So is her hair. White blond, I think they call it. With a curt nod at my father, she turns toward me.

"This is Sam, my daughter," Dad says.

I should be used to it by now—that glassy-eyed look that means whoever is wearing it is trying not to be shocked. The thing is that apart from my curly black hair and light brown skin, I'm the spitting image of my blond father—right down to my slender nose, high cheekbones, and blue eyes.

Yes, blue.

Mom's an anthropologist. She's done all sorts of research on this and has discovered that blue eyes on black people trace back to one single ancestor from ten thousand years ago who lived just north of the Black Sea, which would mean in Ukraine now, but I doubt they called it that back then. Mom has brown eyes, not blue, but she passed the blue-eyed gene or DNA or whatever it is onto me. The tight-lipped woman recovers almost immediately.

"Nice to meet you, Sam," she says.

Dad's friend fires off questions about old classmates with WASP-y names like Thumper and Chip as he guides us through a marble foyer and up a curving marble staircase that looks as if it came from *Gone with the Wind*. At the top is a wide hallway.

On both sides, portraits of stern looking people gaze down at me from ornate gold frames. Among the uniformed patriarchs and sour-faced women is a pretty girl about my age wearing a pert little hat with blue flowers and green ribbons.

The hat is crooked, and I'm itching to reach out and straighten it.

"Who's that?" I say.

No answer from the woman whose name Dad whispered to me but I cannot now remember. She just gives an exasperated cluck and urges me forward.

My room is the first one on the right. It overlooks the front driveway. Behind the ornamental pond and a well-clipped hedge is the barn, and I can't wait to get there.

But first, I am told to rest.

"You've had a long journey," the woman says.

She nods toward a four-poster bed with a lace canopy fluttering in the breeze from a window fan—no air conditioning—that's moving warm air from one part of the room to another.

"The bathroom's over there," she says, pointing.

I remember my manners. "Thank you."

"My daughter, Carrie, will be home soon," says the woman. "She's at a play rehearsal."

"Cool," I say. "What play?"

"*Little Women.*"

6

CAROLINE

Mississippi, July 1863

THEO'S MOOD LIGHTENS when we leave the hayloft. In the harness room he picks up my side saddle. I shake my head.

"I have other plans."

"Going bareback again?"

"No, I'm going to use this." I pull my father's McClellan saddle off its rack. We have to keep quiet about its name because General McClellan is a Yankee, but the saddle he designed is used by soldiers on both sides and it's way more comfortable than the saddles they were issued.

"You like to live dangerously," Theo says.

"I'm already in hot water."

"You shouldn't have gone swimming in the duck pond."

"No," I say. "I shouldn't have been caught."

Theo laughs. "Fair enough, but remember how Mama feels about ladies who ride astride." He gathers up his own saddle. "And she's not the only one. Think of all the other tongues that will start wagging when our neighbors see you riding like a farmer's son."

If Papa were here he'd forbid me to brush Pandora myself. But he's not here, so I dismiss the two barn slaves and groom my horse without help.

In less than ten minutes, I am covered with dirt. My fingernails are black, bits of straw bedding cling to my legs, and the holes in Theo's breeches have grown larger. My hair, no doubt, resembles a bird's nest—it usually does, even without provocation.

Wiping my face with the tails of my brother's old shirt, I stand back to admire my handiwork. Pandora looks more like a bronze statue than a real horse. Sunlight from the stall window dances across her shoulders and hindquarters, highlighting those muscles I'm not supposed to think about. Her mane ripples like black water down her neck. The tiny diamond on her forehead is startlingly white.

I love all the horses here, but Pandora is special. I watched her being born. Back then, I still believed that babies, including foals, were delivered by storks. But while peering through the hayloft's floorboards, I discovered it was just another fairytale, like Santa Claus and the Tooth Fairy.

Theo yells at me to hurry up.

Mounted on Meteor, the barn's fastest gelding, my brother wears a buckskin vest with fringe and laces and Indian beads that a frontiersman gave Papa many years ago. I've always yearned for that vest, but it would be more than my life is worth to borrow it. I'm just lucky to have Theo's old breeches and his linen shirts.

And his silence.

Gently, I place Papa's saddle on Pandora's broad back, slip on her bridle, and fasten the throat latch. Then I lead my mare outside and she stands perfectly still while I swing myself into the saddle.

It feels good to have both legs wrapped around a horse. Apart from my disaster in the duck pond, I haven't ridden astride in over a month.

"I'm ready," I say, holding the reins with one hand and shielding my eyes with the other. It's barely nine o'clock, but already the air is heavy with heat.

"Where shall we ride?" Theo says.

"How about the racetrack?"

"That's asking for failure," he says. "I'll only beat you."

"Not this time, Theo Chandler," I say, patting Pandora's neck. "It's our turn to win."

On our way to the track we pass a line of slaves—men, women, and children—heading off to the cotton fields. The slaves are shabbily dressed and some are barefoot as they shuffle in front of Zeke Turner, our plantation's overseer. He rides a brown mare and carries a long whip, but it's not only for his horse. I've seen him use it on the slaves.

He tips his straw hat as we ride by.

Theo and I warm up our horses, first at a trot, then a slow canter. We won't gallop until we reach the track. It was built by our father to condition his horses. Most of them compete, and often win, in harness racing, and a couple of our farm's young stallions have gained considerable fame on the flat. Their success has furthered Papa's reputation as one of Mississippi's finest horse breeders. His name, John Chandler, is already whispered about in plantations as far away as Georgia and South Carolina.

"Ready when you are," Theo says.

I shorten my reins and grip Papa's saddle with my knees. Sensing what's coming next, Pandora skitters sideways. She loves to race and so do I. But more than that, I love to beat Theo. This time, we will win.

"Let's go!" I shout.

The wind whips my words away as Pandora leaps forward. I crouch over her neck and feel the power in her body. Matching Meteor stride for stride, my wonderful horse gives it everything she has. Legs pounding, she eats up the turf. At the end of one circuit, we're in the lead by a nose.

I urge Pandora even faster.

My hair, now completely loose from its braid, slashes my face. The sound of hoofbeats batters my ears. Leaning forward, I yell to Pandora and get a mouth full of flying mane.

This is the best feeling in the world—riding a horse that nobody else can. And because of this, Pandora is safe. No soldier can take her away. We're now two lengths ahead of Theo and coming around for the second time when I see him—a tall man with a top hat riding toward us on a black horse.

What's Papa doing here?

What's brought him home so early? Has he received bad news about the war? Or have I so totally lost track of time that it's now midafternoon? Slowing down, I squint into the sun. But no, it can't be any later than ten, eleven at the most.

My brother's chestnut gelding surges past us, but the race doesn't matter any more. What matters is the reason for Papa's unexpected return.

He's not riding Raven, his favorite stallion. He's riding Celeste, one of our carriage horses. The black mare is still in her harness, traces hanging loose by her sweaty sides.

I stare at my father.

His frock coat is dusty, his trousers are torn, and he's sitting awkwardly behind Celeste's leather surcingle.

"What happened?" I say. "Why are you riding like that?"

"Seems to me I should be asking you the same question," Papa says, looking at me. "Isn't that my saddle and aren't those Theo's breeches?" He takes off his hat and tries to wipe off the dust with his sleeve, but it doesn't do any good. "And why did you leave the house without permission?"

"Because I had to see Pandora," I say, patting her neck. "I had to say goodbye before going away."

"Even if it meant disobeying your mother?"

"She doesn't understand horses."

"Maybe not," Papa says, "but she does understand the need for propriety. She's strict with you because it's in your best interests." His tone softens. "You can't be running around like a tomboy forever."

My brother rides up.

Meteor's sides are heaving. "Father, what's wrong?" Theo says. "Why are you back so early?"

"We hit a patch of rough road and the carriage broke an axle," Papa says, replacing his hat. "Your mother and I rode the horses back home."

It takes a few seconds for this to sink in. My mother, Harriet Clay Chandler, has ridden astride? Bareback? I suck in my breath. This is unbelievable, but then again, my mother probably didn't have a choice. She and Papa wouldn't have had saddles with them in the carriage. Poor Mama. She must have been mortified. I bite back a smile, not daring to look at my brother.

He says, "Can I do anything to help?"

"You can go and make sure someone's arranged to pick up my carriage," Papa says.

"Yes, sir," Theo says and takes off.

Dirt flies from Meteor's hooves as he thunders down the path between our cotton fields. Some of the Negroes stop whatever it is they're doing to watch. The overseer cracks his whip. The slaves go back to work, and in no time at all my brother is just a speck in the distance.

Papa turns his full attention on me. "First of all, you're going to clean yourself up, find some presentable clothes, and make peace with your mother."

I know better than to argue. "Yes, Papa."

"Then you're going to apologize to your sister for making such a fuss about that dress."

"It wasn't the dress, it was the corset," I say, trying not to flinch because I can still imagine it digging into me. "It's got more bones than a catfish."

Papa's mouth forms the hint of a smile. "You can't always have what you want, Caroline," he says. "Life doesn't work that way."

"I'll die if they make me wear it."

"Caroline, that's enough. I'm in no mood for melodrama," Papa says and gathers up his reins. Celeste gives an impatient little sigh, as if she's not in the mood either. "Just do what I say," my father goes on, "and I won't tell Mama you've been riding in your brother's breeches. She's had enough shocks for one day."

7

SAMANTHA

Mississippi, present day

DESPITE THE BATHROOM'S fancy gold fixtures that look as if they came from another century, I get hot water from the shower and there are plenty of huge fluffy towels to dry myself with.

Winged cherubs watch me from the ceiling.

Totally weird.

Before we left, Mom told me that many big southern houses didn't survive the Civil War, but this one obviously did. It's old, but not as old as our farm in Connecticut that goes back to the early 1700s. There are no cherubs, winged or otherwise, on the ceilings at home—just plain old plaster and white paint. My phone buzzes.

A text from Jenna: *where r u?*

chatting up a cherub
in heaven?
I roll my eyes. *too hot*
lol.

Wrapped in a towel, I rummage in my suitcase for the oversized tank top I like to sleep in. On the front it says *Barn Bratz*, so I pull it on, and I'm about to climb into bed when I notice something wedged between two floorboards.

It looks like a coin.

Sacrificing two finger nails, I manage to pry it out. It's a dime, I think, but given all the tarnish and dirt, it's hard to tell. Its edges are smooth, almost like a penny, but it's smaller so I figure it has to be a dime. I'll give it to Mom. She collects old coins, and I seriously doubt the owners of Heritage Meadows would miss it.

Standing up, I turn to the bed.

It's tall enough to need a mounting block. The pillows are soft, the mattress is super comfortable, and it feels kind of weird, lying on memory foam from the twenty-first century and looking up at a lace canopy that's got to be a hundred years old. Maybe older. I wonder if that girl in the fancy hat ever slept here.

Nahh . . . this bed couldn't be *that* old.

Pushing the down comforter to one side, I hold up the dime. It feels cool against my fingers, almost tingly. I give it a little rub. Some of the grime flakes off.

Wow.

I didn't expect that.

I turn the dime and rub it a bit more, feeling like Aladdin

and his lamp. But nothing happens. No genie wafts out in front of me, all blue and wispy looking and offering me three wishes like the Disney film promised. But I am a little sleepy. We got up at four thirty this morning to make our flight. It's now three in the afternoon.

Quickly, I fire off another text to Jenna, then plug in my earbuds and click on my playlist. A few Lady Gagas will take me right away from Heritage Meadows and having to be downstairs in a skirt and acting like a young lady. Oh, and meeting Carrie.

I hope she's not a total nerd.

8

CAROLINE

Mississippi, July 1863

STILL WEARING THEO'S BREECHES, I sneak into the house through the kitchen door and race up the servants' narrow stairs to my bedroom.

Slaves with hooded eyes watch as I fly by.

Mama's maid gives a loud, "Tut-tut," but it doesn't matter any more. Everyone, down to the lowliest field hand, knows I'm in serious trouble.

To keep Mama happy I wash my hands and face and re-braid my hair. Then I strip off Theo's breeches and pull my best summer dress from the armoire. The skirt is green-and-white paisley; the bodice is dark green with a white collar and tiny pearl buttons up the front. It has huge over-sleeves that Mama says are the latest fashion. At supper they drip into your soup if you're not careful.

But first come the pantalettes, a white chemise, and one white petticoat—but no corset and no hoop.

I despise hoops.

It's like having your legs trapped inside a giant bird cage. You can't sit down or walk through narrow doors because your crinoline gets in the way. Some ladies, like my mother and sister, wear four or five petticoats over their hoops so the whalebone rings won't show through the delicate silk of their dresses.

I glance down at my feet.

I'm still wearing my boots. The tops are clean but the soles are covered in manure. I wipe most of it off with a rag that a slave has left beneath my bed. I sniff.

My boots are still smelly.

Maybe a little scent would help. I have some here somewhere. Louise gave me a bottle of her favorite, but I've never used it. She said it was called *Camellia* and came from our great-aunt Maude, who lives in New Orleans. That's way south of here.

Amid the muddle of books, ivory combs, and tortoiseshell hair clips on my dresser I find Louise's bottle behind my jar of coins and sprinkle perfume over my boots. Then, just to be sure, I sprinkle some over myself. I now smell like Papa's greenhouse where he grows orchids and, I suppose, camellias. Before leaving my room, I wrap my shoulders in a fringed shawl. It's far too hot for a shawl, but it might make Mama feel as if I'm really trying.

Her parlor is on the first floor and it's filled to the brim with porcelain figurines, uncomfortable chairs, and spindly-legged tables holding English tea cups that nobody ever drinks out of.

My maternal grandmother, Abigail Clay, peers at me dis-
approvingly from a gilt frame above the marble fireplace.
Even though it's just past midday, hardly any light shines
through Mama's tall windows, thanks to her heavy velvet
drapes that keep most of it out.

After Mama delivers her usual lecture about my need to
grow up and take responsibility for my actions, she tells me to
go and find my sister. So I do because there's no point in
making Mama angrier than she already is.

Louise is still in bed. She rarely gets up before noon.

"I'm sorry about the dress, and I promise to wear it," I
say, approaching my sister's four-poster bed. Its white canopy
has silk tassels the size of my fist. "But I refuse to wear that
horrible corset." I look at the shape curled up beneath a
tangle of sheets. "Louise, did you hear me?"

My sister's delicate face is flushed with sleep. Her lemony-
fresh hair fans across the pillow. I touch her shoulder, and
Louise's blue eyes flutter open.

She yawns. "What time is it?"

"Almost noon."

"Oh, it's still early." Louise closes her eyes, then opens
them again. "What did you say?"

"Almost noon."

"No, before that."

"I'll wear the dress."

"You will?"

"But not the corset."

"You don't need one anyway," Louise says. She sits up
and smiles. "You'll be the prettiest bridesmaid at my wedding. Much prettier than Alice."

I groan. "I'm supposed to be packing."

"Where are you going?"

"Mama's sending me to the Hamiltons'."

"Then she obviously doesn't think you've had enough punishment," Louise says, swinging her legs over the bed. Her cotton shift has more ruffles and satin ribbons than I can count. "You'd better get ready."

"What should I take?"

Louise raises an eyebrow. "Tell your maid to do it."

"I don't have one, remember?"

"So, get another," Louise says airily.

I'll ask Mama to give me Pearl. We're obliged to bring a personal maid when we go visiting our neighbors' plantations—except Pearl is so new that she won't know what I'm supposed to pack any more than I do.

Sensing my dilemma, Louise says, "Then I'll come and supervise. Just give me a few minutes."

This will take an hour.

First my sister will have to summon help with getting dressed; then it'll be her hair and just the right pair of shoes. After that she'll open her enormous armoire and choose the cast-off dresses, petticoats, and bonnets that she thinks are suitable for me to take.

By the time Louise gets to my bedroom, it will be dark and I'll be long gone—doing penance at the Hamiltons' for all the sins I've committed. The only one who'll have a good time is Pearl. She'll get to sleep in my room and gossip with the Hamiltons' slaves. I bet they say dreadful things about us.

I dawdle along the hall.

Off to my left is the staircase I ran down this morning. I'd give anything to be running down it again, racing outside and into freedom.

But here in the South, girls don't have freedom. We're locked into corsets and crinolines, we're not allowed to say what we think, and we're forced to pose for portraits like the ones Mama commissioned a famous artist to paint of Louise and me last year—except Louise's now hangs above the sideboard in our dining room while mine has been banished to the upstairs hall.

As I pass it, I poke out my tongue.

Secretly, I am longing for the day when my portrait pokes out its tongue at me. The other portraits are frowny; at least mine is smiling. Not that I felt like smiling as I posed for it, hour after hour wearing that silly little hat.

The door to my room is closed. Still thinking about freedom I open it. And there, on my bed, is a half-naked slave fast asleep with a tiny book on her chest and strings leading into both ears. Faintly, I hear music.

At least, I *think* it's music.

~9~

SAMANTHA

Mississippi . . .

SOMEONE SHAKES ME.

No, no, says my dream.

I don't want to wake up. I'm about to jump Nugget over the sculptured hedges that surround Heritage Meadows. We gallop toward them. I lean into Nugget's mane, and . . .

"Get out," someone yells.

Out of what?

Totally confused, I push Nugget forward, but he's fading before my eyes—first his ears, then his neck and withers—until I'm left with nothing except a pounding heart and this person, whoever it is, shaking me as if I were a rag doll.

I open one eye, then the other.

Leaning over me is a girl wearing old-fashioned clothes—

a long green skirt, a fringed shawl, and a tight-fitting blouse with buttons up the front. A tiny gold locket dangles from a chain around her neck. This must be Carrie. She's home from her *Little Women* play practice. I guess it was a dress rehearsal.

"Hi," I say.

For a moment, we stare at one another. She takes a step backward as I yank out my earbuds. My tank top has ridden up, so I pull it down because I'd forgotten to put on my underpants.

Whoops.

"Sorry," I say, covering myself with the sheet.

It feels different from the one I went to sleep with. So does the down comforter that I'd shoved to one side. It's morphed into a cotton quilt like the ones my grandmother used to make. I even recognize a couple of squares—"Jacob's Ladder" and "Churn Dash," though how they got those peculiar names is beyond me.

Carrie's mouth opens, then closes.

She says, "How dare you?"

Huh?

"Didn't your mom tell you I'd be staying over?" I say.

Climbing off the bed, I look around for my suitcase. I need underwear, and fast, but my luggage has disappeared. So I rip the sheet off the bed and wrap myself in it.

I turn toward Carrie.

She's still staring at me like I'm an alien from another planet. Mom said that some people in the South could be kind of peculiar about biracial kids, but this is a bit more than I expected. Maybe horses will work.

"Do you ride?" I say.

She gulps. "Yes."

"What's your horse's name?"

This always helps to break the ice. No matter who you're talking to, if they love horses you can get beyond whatever barriers you think are out there if you share your horses' names.

"Pandora," she says.

"Mine is Nugget."

"But you're a slave," she says. "Slaves don't own horses."

"This one does," I say, holding up my hand for a high five. But Carrie doesn't respond. I guess she's still in *Little Women* mode. "I'm a slave in the barn and for my father. He's, like, totally ruthless about my riding."

From outside come voices, men's voices.

Trying not to trip over my sheet, I hobble to the window and peer out. Two guys are circling on horseback. The older man wears a top hat and striped pants. The younger one is blond and bare-headed. His fringed vest reminds me of the ones that Western riders wear. I guess he and the other man came home with Carrie from her *Little Women* rehearsal.

Riding horses?

If my school put on plays like this where you could ride horses, I'd be all over it, never mind I can't act or carry a tune in a bucket—much to my mother's disappointment. She's starred in so many local musicals that I've lost count.

Sweat trickles down my face.

Wasn't there a fan in this window when I went to sleep? I move the lace curtains to one side—I don't remember those either—and take another look at the sweeping gravel driveway. Except it's not gravel any more; it's plain dirt with lots of ruts.

And where is our rental car?

Okay, it was uglier than sin so maybe Hughie-Dewey told my dad to take it around the back so nobody would see it. I'm totally on board with that. I wouldn't want that awful car cluttering up my elegant front garden, either.

But right now, all I see is a four-wheeled carriage tilting to one side like an axle is broken. Maybe this is a stage prop that Carrie's dad is going to work on. Our high school's drama club did *Little Women* last year, but all they had was a carriage painted on a backdrop.

I rub my eyes and look again.

What happened to the tunnel of live oak that Dad and I drove through? The trees I'm looking at now are less than ten feet tall. Did they turn into saplings while I was asleep? They're so thin and spindly I can see all the way to the end of the farm's driveway.

I guess I was more tired than I thought, and now I can't seem to wake up properly. There's a knock at the door.

Oh great, more visitors.

⤳ 10 ⤳

CAROLINE

Mississippi, July 1863

WRAPPED IN A SHEET—*my sheet*—the slave girl says, "I guess you'd better open it."

Her voice sounds odd, like it doesn't belong around here. She stares at me as if we're equals, the way Pearl did downstairs.

"Caroline," says my sister's voice. "Open the door."

This means that Louise has her arms full of clothes I don't want and that she can't open the door herself, otherwise she'd come right in the way she always does.

Last week she caught me reading one of Papa's horse anatomy books. I snuffed out my oil lamp so fast, it fell over and broke the chimney. Luckily that was enough to distract Louise from my stolen book, and I was able to hide it beneath my quilt.

Louise knocks again.

Nervously, I glance at the door then turn to look at the slave, but her back is toward me and she's peering out the window, nose pressed to the glass like she wants to eat it.

"Nice horses," she says. "They're gorgeous."

"Yes," I reply.

What am I thinking?

Talking to a slave about horses? I should be shoving her out of my room and yelling at her for sleeping in my bed, then dispatching her down to the kitchen where our housekeeper will probably beat her.

But I can't.

Why?

Something about her intrigues me. My sister bangs on the door again.

"Go away," I yell. "I've got a headache."

"I'm sorry," Louise says. "Shall I call Mama?"

That's the last thing I need. "No, I'll be all right. Just let me rest."

I hold my breath and hope Louise doesn't suddenly remember that I never get headaches, nor do I ever need to rest. From behind the door there's a sigh, and I can just imagine my sister's pursed lips—so like our mother's—and her puzzled frown as she tries to sort it all out. The slave girl turns toward me.

"Are you okay?" she says.

What does *that* mean?

Why is she asking me about two letters in the alphabet? It makes no sense.

But neither does she.

Her eyes, I've just noticed, are blue and slaves don't have blue eyes. They don't have sharp tongues either, but this one does. Taking a step backward, I reach behind me, fumble for the key, and lock my bedroom door. For some reason I can't explain I don't want anyone to come in.

❧ 11 ❧

SAMANTHA

Mississippi . . .

STILL CLUTCHING THE SHEET, I look again for my
suitcase. I left it on a low table, but in its place is a tall
wooden cupboard I don't remember seeing before.

This whole room is different.

When I went to sleep, the walls were plain white . . . I'm
sure they were. Now they're covered in red wallpaper. It has
stripes and squiggly bits and I get dizzy just looking at them.
Have I entered some sort of time warp?

"Who *are* you?" I say to Carrie.

She counters with, "Who are *you*?"

"My name is Samantha DeVries," I say. "But most people
call me Sam."

"That's a boy's name."

"So?"

We stare at one another. Her eyes are the color of spring grass and they're boring into me like a dentist's drill.

"I'm Caroline Chandler," she finally says.

"Carrie?"

"No, Caroline."

She tugs at her skirt as if it's bothering her, then unlaces her boots and kicks them off. I get a whiff of horse manure mixed with something sweet and faintly exotic.

Perfume?

This whole thing is freaking me out. It's like I just stepped into one of my brother's time travel books, but those aren't real. They're fiction and they're totally off the wall. "Okay," I say, deciding to play along. "What year is it?"

"It's eighteen sixty-three," she says. "Everyone knows that."

"Yeah, right," I say. "In *Little Women* it is."

This much I remember from reading it. The father was involved in the Civil War, the mother was called Marmee, and the four sisters were always squabbling with each other. One was a writer; another was mad for boys.

Or something.

Jenna needs to hear about this, like right now. I grab my iPhone and punch in a text:

Am stuck in Little Women, w/o panties. HELP!

The minute I hit *send*, up comes a warning that says *Not Delivered*. My battery is charged, but there are no bars. None. I had four earlier. I guess the cell service is down.

Caroline points. "What *is* that?"

"An iPhone."

Is she totally stupid or is she one of those stubborn idiots who refuse to buy an Apple product no matter how good it is? My dad was like that until I convinced him that iPhones were the best. Now he's got a MacBook Air, the latest iPad, and—

There's another knock on the door. Softer this time.

Caroline says, "Who's there?"

"Pearl," comes the reply.

Opening the door a couple of inches, Caroline leans toward it as if she's on a secret mission. There's a whispered conversation, but I can't hear what they're saying.

And who is Pearl?

It sounds really old fashioned, like Ruby and Opal. None of my friends has a name like that.

12

CAROLINE

Mississippi, July 1863

WITH ANOTHER GLANCE at the half-dressed slave girl, I tell Pearl to bring me her spare clothes.

"I don't have any," she whispers.

Slaves aren't supposed to argue. They're supposed to obey. I grab Pearl's arm and pull her into my room, and now I've got two slave girls looking at me as if I am half mad.

Locking the door, I wonder how I could have gotten myself into this ridiculous mess—a slave girl wrapped in my bed sheet and another who's bold enough to challenge me, never mind my sister who could be summoning my mother at any minute.

I decide to take charge.

"Sit down." I point to my bed.

It's easier to command slaves when you're taller than they are, even though Mama says they're not supposed to sit in your presence. But this time I don't care. I doubt my parents have ever encountered a situation like this, and I seriously doubt that Theo has, either.

Obediently, both girls sit.

"You," I say to Pearl. "Go back downstairs and find me another set of clothes, just like yours, and don't tell anyone about it."

"Yes, ma'am."

Scrambling to her feet, Pearl scuttles toward my door. I open it, then lock it behind her. The other girl fiddles with her tiny book. I lean closer, curious to see what she's doing.

"Show me that."

"Sure," she says, handing it to me.

It's nothing like I've ever seen before. It's the same shape as the small diary I keep, and it weighs about the same, but that's where the similarity ends. I can't even begin to describe it.

"What *is* this?" I say to her.

❧ 13 ❧

SAMANTHA

Mississippi . . .

"IT'S A CELL PHONE," I say. "Haven't you ever seen one before?"

"No," Caroline says.

But it's hard to believe.

Cell phones are all over the world, like in Tibet and Borneo and the Amazon jungle. Even people in Africa with no electricity and running water have cell phones these days.

You can't get away from them.

My mother says they're a plague, that we'd be better off without them because people who text friends in front of you when you're trying to have a friendly conversation with them are diabolically rude.

Her words, not mine.

But what Mom doesn't realize is that I need to be in touch with my friends, like all the time.

Gently, I take my phone from Caroline's hands and try texting Jenna again, but get the same message as before. Okay, so the lines aren't working; maybe the web is. I hit Google and get a gray screen—*Safari cannot open the page, blah, blah, blah, because your iPhone is not connected to the Internet.*

That's when it hits me.

Those guys outside on their horses, the broken carriage, the spindly trees that ought to be eighty feet tall . . . and Caroline's genuinely puzzled expression.

This is *not* a play.

It's not *Little Women*. It's real life and it's happening right now. I am in another world. Okay, I'm willing to buy that . . . for now.

But how did I get here?

Even more important, how do I get back home?

I'm still trying to process all this when Pearl returns. With a nod at Caroline, she drops an armload of clothes on the bed—a long brown skirt, a homespun blouse, and a pair of lace-up boots. No underwear, though, and that's what I desperately need. I can't float about all weekend with no bra and no panties.

Pearl gives me an odd look, then quietly leaves the room. It's almost as if she hasn't even been here.

I reach for the skirt.

It feels rough, like a burlap grain sack from years ago before they began using plastic. I look closer. It *is* an old grain sack. Bits of wheat, or maybe they're oats, hide between the fibers. This is not something I'd put on, even in my most desperate moments. I always wear my socks and underpants inside-out because the seams annoy me.

"Don't you have any jeans?" I say.

"Jean?" Caroline says. "Who's she?"

At this point, my patience runs out, and I don't care what world I'm in—mine, hers, or two thousand years from now. I leap off the bed, scattering boots and clothes, and dive for that tall wooden cupboard where my suitcase should have been. I bet it's full of useful stuff like shirts, pants, and breeches.

I yank open a door.

But the cupboard is crammed with gowns—golden yellow, emerald green, light blue, and deep red—that look more like theatre costumes than anything a normal girl would wear.

Caroline slams the door.

"Yikes." I pull my hand away just in time.

She says, "You can't wear my clothes."

"Why?"

Not that I want to, but her dresses look way more comfortable than the burlap skirt and peasant blouse that would probably itch me to death. Never mind those tiny boots that my big feet would never fit into.

"Because . . . because you're a slave."

"*Not*," I say.

Our eyes lock again. I won't blink until she does. We're standing so close our noses almost touch. I see the freckles across her pale cheeks, the gold flecks in her irises, and the way her mouth turns up at the corners as if she's just thought of something funny.

She says, "You have blue eyes."

"And yours are green," I say.

She blinks.

"Okay," I say, feeling like a winner. "Now that we've gotten this out of the way, may I please borrow some underpants? I promise to wash them before giving them back."

I tug at my sheet, but the other end has gotten wrapped around the bedpost. I risk another vicious tug and it comes loose so fast I almost fall over.

Caroline gives a muffled snort.

"Look, I can't wear this sheet all weekend," I say, "so I really do need some underwear or whatever you call it."

She sighs. "All right."

From a drawer she pulls out a couple of old garments that Little Bo Peep might have worn—a long white shift and a pair of baggy bloomers with rows of lace and thin satin ribbons instead of elastic. Caroline has to be dreaming if she thinks I'll wear these. On the other hand, I don't seem to have much choice.

She turns away, as if embarrassed to watch me get dressed. I can't imagine the girls at school doing this. We share changing rooms and showers, and everyone knows what size boobs you have—big, small, or some place in between.

Mine are flatter than pancakes, which is great for riding. You don't want them bouncing up and down in front of you like a pair of tennis balls. Most of the time, I don't even need a bra, but Mom makes me wear a sports bra, just to be more comfortable.

I wish I had one with me.

There were two in my suitcase, but that has definitely disappeared, along with my knapsack and Nugget's pedigree. All I possess in whatever world I'm in right now are my earbuds and iPhone, my *Barn Bratz* tank top, and that dime I dug out of the floorboards. It's a lot shinier now than when I found it, and I'm flipping it over to read the date when Caroline grabs it.

"That's mine," I say.

"No, it's mine," she says.

But before I have a chance to object, Caroline crosses the room to her dresser and drops my dime into a glass jar. It tinkles against the other coins in there. I guess this is her piggy bank.

That's when I spy the breeches.

They're lying in a messy heap at the foot of my bed. Ditching the lace bloomers, I drop my sheet and snatch up the breeches.

"No," Caroline shouts.

"Why not?" I say, pulling them on. They fit pretty well despite being baggy in the seat. They're also stained and ripped, just like mine at home. I fasten the front buttons—no zipper—but at this point I don't care.

"They're my brother's," Caroline says.

"So?"

"Girls don't wear breeches."

"Then what are they doing in your room?"

Caroline opens her mouth and shuts it. Yet again, we stare at one another like an old comedy routine—think Abbott and Costello or Laurel and Hardy. Pretty soon we'll turn into Bart and Lisa Simpson.

There's a long silence.

Footsteps pad down the hall, but nobody stops to knock on our door. I have a feeling that if they did stop, Caroline would yell at them to go away. I've already figured out that we're in a time warp, so what can I do to convince Caroline as well?

All I have is my iPhone. "Do you know what a photograph is?" I ask Caroline.

She puts a hand to her locket. "Yes."

"Okay," I say, "then here are some photos of my family."

"But—"

"Ignore my iPhone," I say. "I'll tell you about that in a minute."

Yeah, right.

How do you explain twenty-first-century technology to a girl who's probably never seen a train before? I wrack my brains, but I can't remember when trains were invented. And have I actually accepted the fact that I've time traveled back to the middle 1800s? This is a mess.

A hot mess.

I take a deep breath and begin scrolling. "That's my dad," I say. "And this is my brother Erik."

"But they're white," Caroline says. "And you're black."

"So is my mother."

"Is she a slave?"

"No."

Caroline coils up her face like a corkscrew. Her hand brushes against mine, and as we touch, she trembles. I get the feeling that this a really big deal for her—like she's never actually touched a black person before, at least, not in friendship.

"Tell me again," I say. "What year is it?"

"Eighteen sixty-three."

It's the middle of the Civil War and we're in Mississippi. I'm from the North, which means Caroline and I are enemies.

This is a bigger mess than I thought.

If only I'd paid more attention to Mom's history lessons. But I didn't. I come from a privileged world of private schools, expensive horses, and people who don't care what color you are as long as you know how to ride and win ribbons.

In our country club circle, I'm a minor celebrity. Members suck up to my dad; then they fawn over me because some of them believe I'll be in the Olympics one day—*I knew Samantha DeVries back when she was in walk-trot classes, and just look at her now!*

Well, I've got news for them.

At the rate things are going, it doesn't look as if the Olympics are in my future. Neither is the next century or the one after. That's when I remember the trees.

"Look at this," I say, flipping to the photo I took when Dad and I came down the driveway.

"That's *my* house," Caroline says.

"It sure is," I say.

Looking at it again, I can still imagine the sleek Jags and Mercedes pulling up beneath the porte cochère to disgorge glamorous people. I can even imagine coaches and horses.

"But—" Caroline falters.

"I took this photo a couple of hours ago, in *my* time," I say. "These trees are huge and amazing, but in *your* time, they're tiny. When did your father plant them?"

"Five years ago."

"Which means," I say, doing some rapid math, "that in my world they're more than a hundred and fifty years old."

For a moment, we just sit there—two girls on a bed in eighteen-whatever-it-is, trying to wrap our arms around this. For her, it's tougher because the only proof I have of being from another century is my iPhone. Her proof is all around me—all have to do is look at it.

She says, "I've read a story about this."

"Time travel?" I say.

"Is that what you call it?"

I nod. "My brother is passionate about it."

"What's his name?"

"Erik," I say. "He's nineteen."

"Mine is Theo," she says. "He's sixteen."

Okay, so here's another connection: We both have brothers, and we both have horses. I can't wait to meet hers. But first, I need to get dressed in something that won't make me stand out like a lawn jockey on top of a wedding cake. I hold up the white undergarment that Caroline gave me.

"What did you say these were called?"

"I didn't," she says. "But we call them drawers."

"Like in a dresser?"

"No, as in bloomers," she says.

Vaguely I remember Mom telling me about a woman called Amelia Bloomer and her campaign for comfortable women's clothing that shocked everyone in the mid-nineteenth century. Then another word from that era flies into my head.

"Unmentionables?" I say.

Caroline covers her mouth with both hands, but her giggles escape anyway, and I get the odd feeling that we're going to be friends—that is, if a black girl and a white girl can be friends in the middle of a Civil War that's divided their country.

I'm beginning to wish I hadn't blown off my history lessons. I have no clue what's supposed to happen next.

But Caroline does.

≈ 14 ≈

CAROLINE

Mississippi, July 1863

WITHOUT THINKING TWICE, I tell Sam to take off Theo's breeches and put on the drawers and chemise I've given her. It feels really strange, calling her Sam, but it suits her better than Samantha does.

"Okay," she says.

"Wait a minute," I say. "What does that mean?"

She shrugs. "Just that it's *okay*, like it's *all right*."

"Acceptable?" I suggest.

"That works for me," Sam replies.

Tucking this into my memory bank, I fling open the armoire. Most of my gowns once belonged to Louise, and I don't like any of them—too many bows, ribbons, and flounces—but that's what Sam and I have to choose from. Between us we have to figure out what dresses, shoes, and hats I need to take to the Hamiltons' house. It's a bewildering assortment, and I hardly know where to begin.

Maybe I really do need Louise's help.

Bad idea.

My sister would ask all sorts of questions about Sam, like where did she come from and why does she have blue eyes, and I'm not ready to answer those.

I don't think Sam is, either.

"Do you actually wear this stuff?" she says, reaching for a white gown trimmed with elaborate pink embroidery and silk rosebuds that my mother is particularly fond of.

And I nod, because I do wear them.

I have no choice.

"This, too?" she says, staring at my crinoline beside the armoire. It stands up all by itself, its network of webbing and rings like a giant empty cage waiting to trap someone—namely, me—inside it.

"Yes," I say, "when Mama forces me."

"What's it made of?" Sam asks.

"Steel rings," I say. "But some are whalebone."

She looks at me, eyes wide with horror. "But that's against the law. You can't kill whales any more. They're protected. Sperm whales are almost extinct. They've been hunted to death for—"

"This?" I say, picking up my oil lamp.

It's not on now, of course, but later, just before it gets dark, the housekeeper will go through our house turning on the lamps. Sometimes we use candles, but they're messy and they drip all over everything, despite their brass holders.

Mama says candles are dangerous.

We almost had a fire last year when a beeswax candle fell onto her carpet and nobody noticed until it began to smoke. Mama has been begging Papa for gas lamps, but he says they're not available here; you can only get them in the cities.

Lamps without oil?

It sounds as fantastic as the horseless carriages and flying machines I've learned about from that book in Papa's library. I ask if Sam knows about them.

"Hell, yes," she says.

And I gasp because that's a word we never use around here. Not in the house, anyway. Theo says it in the barn all the time, and even the grooms roll their eyes at him. Mama would faint if she heard me say it, and I'd be banned from church. But coming from Sam, it seems almost natural. It rolls off her tongue the way *pantaloons* and *chemise* roll off mine.

"Tell me," I say.

It's still early afternoon, so we have plenty of time, and I listen, totally spellbound, as Sam describes her amazing world. She shows me pictures on this thing she calls an iPhone.

"Here's Nugget," Sam says.

Most of what she tells me is incomprehensible, but this I can understand—a beautiful chestnut with a flaxen mane and tail. We don't often see horses this color, but whenever they show up, people go a little crazy over them. I think Mr. Hamilton has a horse like this. I make a mental note to show Sam when we get there.

But will I be allowed to?

She'll be acting as my maid, not as a companion. I won't

be able to take Sam into the Hamiltons' barn without a dozen pairs of eyebrows being raised, never mind the social drums that will reach my mother faster than a telegraph.

I can't believe how easily I've accepted this. Sam comes from another world. She's totally convinced me of that.

It's terribly exciting. And scary, too.

There's a sharp knock at the door. "Caroline?"

Mama!

That's even more scary.

"Quick, hide," I tell Sam.

"Where?"

I point to the tiny room that I use for personal hygiene. It has winged cherubs on the ceiling and I always feel awkward with those fat little angels looking down at me when I'm doing something private, like using the chamber pot.

Mine is in a commode—a wooden frame that's the height of a chair. And this is why I wish I could wear breeches all the time. It's a whole lot easier to pull them down than to pull up a bunch of petticoats and hooped skirts when you need to relieve yourself.

The minute Sam's out of sight, I take a deep breath and walk to my door. I open it a crack.

Mama says, "Are you getting ready?"

"Of course," I say.

"The Hamiltons' coach will be here at any minute." There's a pause. "I trust you not to let me down, Caroline," Mama says.

"I won't," I say, crossing my fingers.

But who knows what will happen with Sam along? We

could fly to the moon and dance among the stars. We could even travel back to Rome or ancient Greece. I've always wondered if Demeter really did give birth to Arion, a horse. The tutor Mama hired would never answer that question. He always blushed and changed the subject.

"About *Romeo and Juliet*," he would say.

I loathed Shakespeare.

But it was worth more than my life to complain. I had to bow my head and pretend to care about two people, my age, in Italy hundreds of years ago, who misunderstood one another.

They both ended up dead.

15

SAMANTHA

Mississippi, July 1863

I REALLY NEED TO PEE, so I use the pot that's suspended in a weird looking wooden frame. I guess this is what passes for a bathroom these days. Carefully, I balance myself over it, then glance at the ceiling.

"Hi, there," I say. "Remember me?"

The smallest cherub blushes—a trick of the light. But what's not a trick of the light is that there is no way to flush this thing. I look around for a handle, and can't find one. There's nothing to wipe myself with, either, except for a pile of newspaper. Bunching up two pages with headlines about the Battle of Vicksburg, I do the best I can.

It is so *not* comfortable.

"Are you finished?" whispers Caroline.

She must've heard me peeing. "Yes."

There's no place to wash my hands, so I open the door and find Caroline pulling clothes from her cupboard and dumping them into a trunk. On the bed is a blue homespun dress, almost like denim. It has long sleeves with frayed cuffs, a high collar, and two pockets sewn onto the skirt. The stitches are so large and clumsy, even I could have done better. I once tried to hem a pair of shorts and ended up sewing them to my jeans.

"For you," Caroline says, pointing at the dress. "But hurry. Mama says the Hamiltons' coach is waiting."

Coach?

While I climb into the cotton drawers, the long chemise, and a dress that has far too many buttons up the front, Caroline tells me about having to visit her neighbors. They sound even worse than some of our snooty country club members, and I'm so engrossed in Caroline's story about her and Alice Hamilton and their ill-fated tutor that I get the first button wrong, which means all the others are, too. With an exasperated smile, Caroline redoes them.

"Zippers," I say.

She looks at me. "What?"

Do I have a picture of one? There are so many photos and videos on my iPhone, I could run the battery down just showing her.

Battery?

I grab the phone and turn it off. Keeping the battery alive is my ticket to believability or whatever I need to help get myself back to the twenty-first century again. Or is it?

I wish I knew how I got here.

And why?

This dress is killing me. I tug at the collar, but it doesn't do any good. It's worse than last season's ratcatcher that you've just outgrown. I ask if we'll be riding to the Hamiltons' house and Caroline laughs.

"You will be up front with the driver," she says. "And I will sit in the carriage beneath a parasol."

With a flourish, she pops one open.

It's pale yellow—the same color as the dress she is now wearing—and it has so many tassels and scallops that it looks as if it came straight from the pages of *Mother Goose*.

"Keep your head down," Caroline says, opening her door and looking both ways. "Don't let anyone see your eyes."

"Why?"

"Because they're blue."

Oh, right.

"I guess I should've worn brown contacts, then," I say, following her along the wide hallway that looks almost the same as it did two hours ago. "That's you, isn't it?" I say, pointing to the portrait.

"Yes, and hush," Caroline says. "Stay behind and don't talk."

"Cute hat," I mutter.

———⊶⊷———

Somehow, I manage to keep my head down and my mouth shut. We reach the front hall—that hasn't changed much, either—and I almost trip over the trunk that Caroline has just packed. It probably weighs a ton, given all the stuff she shoved into it, including my tank top and her brother's old breeches.

"Whoops," I say, but nobody notices.

Two men wearing baggy pants heft Caroline's trunk into the back of a carriage that waits beneath the porte cochère. The carriage is black and shiny, and it's pulled by two perfectly matched dark bays with white stars and gleaming harnesses. Buckles and bits twinkle as the horses toss their heads.

Their side reins are too tight.

A tall woman glides toward us. Her long purple skirt is the size of a small parachute, and it sways from side to side so smoothly it looks as if she's on roller skates. Maybe she is. I can't see her feet.

"Good-bye, Mama," Caroline says.

"Remember what I told you," the woman says. With a sniff, she glances at me. "Your new maid?"

I close my eyes, hoping she didn't see them.

"Yes, Mama."

"Very well, then."

There are no hugs and kisses, no sign from Caroline's mother that her daughter is going away for five days.

"Tell Louise I said good-bye," Caroline says, gathering up her skirts. She's wearing white gloves—the perfect Southern lady.

"No need," someone chirps.

Without thinking, I turn. So this is Louise. Sweeping past me, she throws her arms around Caroline. "I hope you have a wonderful time, and try not to miss me too much," she says, kissing her sister on both cheeks. Hair the color of Nugget's mane tumbles down her back. Mrs. Chandler scolds her for not pinning it up.

"Sorry, Mama," Louise says.

Then a couple of male voices join in, and all of a sudden it seems as if the entire Chandler clan is here to give Caroline a rousing send-off.

Good thing, too. Otherwise I might forget myself and say something rude to Caroline's mother for being such a witch.

"Give my regards to the Hamiltons," says Caroline's father.

At least, I think that's who it is. His hair is thick and silver, like Hughie-Dewey's, and he has the same booming voice. He commands attention.

So does Theo, but only because he's drop-dead gorgeous, with green eyes, freckles, and a wickedly cute smile. He's shed his Western vest for a formal jacket and starched shirt. Its collar looks about as uncomfortable as mine. I sense him looking at me.

Maybe he's curious.

I'm trying my best to act like a servant, but it's not as easy as you might think. I wonder if Theo suspects anything. He gives Caroline a hug, almost knocking her over. "Don't worry about Pandora," he says. "I'll feed her treats for you."

Mama Chandler makes a noise in her throat. She's even worse than Hughie-Dewey's transparent wife.

I will be *so* glad to get out of here.

———◦∞◦———

Caroline said it's only eight miles to the Hamiltons' plantation, but it takes us forever to get there. I sit up front with the
driver. He seems oblivious to the horses' distress, and I'm
dying to tell him to get off the stupid carriage and loosen their
side reins.

But I can't.

He says, "Where you from?"

"Conn—" I catch myself in time. "No place special."

He shrugs like it really doesn't matter. I feel a poke and
turn around. Caroline frowns at me.

Careful, she mouths.

If we can get through the next twenty-four hours without
me making a huge blunder and blowing my cover, it will be a
serious miracle. I have visions of being locked up . . . or
worse—being flogged.

Mom had tried to make me understand, but I'd tuned her
out because I couldn't cope with it. When slaves step out of
line, even for the silliest little thing, they are severely punished. If only I could figure out how I got here, then I'd be
able to go home.

Is Dad worried about me? Does he even know I've disappeared? How does time happen in the real world when you've
left it and are now somewhere else?

Erik would know.

Without thinking, I pull out my phone.

Another poke from Caroline. Luckily, the driver doesn't
notice. He's too busy avoiding a giant pothole and another
carriage coming toward us. I shove the phone back in my
pocket.

After what I figure has to be another half mile, the Hamiltons' plantation finally comes into view, and I gasp.

Wow!

It's like the movie set for *Gone with the Wind*.

We watched it on Netflix the other night. I thought Scarlett was a stitch, but Mom pointed out that Melanie Wilkes was a much stronger woman. Nicer, too.

"So was Mammy," Erik said.

My mother sighed. "Oh, yes."

16

CAROLINE

Mississippi, July 1863

LIKE A PAIR OF PORCELAIN DOLLS on guard duty, Alice and her mother stand on the front steps. They sweep me into the house in such a hurry that I can't see what happens to Sam. Before we left I tried to warn her what it would be like—sleeping on a pallet in my room and sharing meals with the Hamiltons' slaves. They're not as well-fed as ours are.

"I hope you like grits and collard greens," I said.

Sam pulled a face. "Ugh."

She doesn't understand. I'm not sure I do either, but I'm learning fast. Ever since Sam arrived, I've taken a hard look at my feelings and prejudices and they're a lot different now from what they were this morning. I think Theo would like Sam. When we get home, I'll tell him about her. Somehow we'll find a way for her to ride with us—that is, if she stays long enough.

"You're late," says Mrs. Hamilton. "My guests are waiting." She tells her servants to bring my trunk upstairs, then wrinkles her nose at the sight of my dusty yellow dress. "I suppose that will have to do. There's no time for another outfit."

Inwardly, I groan.

Nothing has changed since my last visit in February. Life at the Hamiltons' is still a nonstop whirl of social engagements. I follow my hostess through the foyer. Alice trots beside her, swathed in a peach-colored gown that does nothing for her sallow complexion.

Perched on brocade and velvet chairs, a group of whiskery old ladies await our arrival in the drawing room. Mrs. Hamilton sits down to pour tea. Spoons tinkle against bone china cups, maids hover with silver trays, and gossip is exchanged. I do my best not to yawn, but this is what I've been dreading—an endless round of parties and soirées that will stretch from now until next Thursday.

Alice seems to thrive on it.

Waddling happily from breakfast to luncheon to seven-course suppers, she acts as though fresh air is dangerous. Once her mother's tea party is over, I try to tempt her outside.

"Shall we go for a ride?"

"Horses make me sneeze."

"Then how about we take a walk?" Feeling trapped, I look through the window. As Louise said, this is merely an extension of my punishment . . . only worse, because now I have Alice to cope with.

"It's too hot," she says, fanning herself.

I try again. "Would you like to play croquet?"

Alice shakes her head.

"Why not?"

"Because Mother doesn't want me out in the sun." Alice pulls at her sleeves until they cover her chubby wrists. "My skin's much too delicate."

"You could always use a parasol."

"But then how would I hold my croquet mallet?"

At this point, all I want to do is smack her with it.

Supper is excruciating, and I wasn't exaggerating about the seven courses, either. Alice devours them as if she were starving, all the way from turtle soup to lemon cake with syllabub.

Her father, Edward Hamilton, spends the entire meal discussing the war with a congressman from Vicksburg and another from Baton Rouge, Louisiana. The women fan themselves and chatter about the latest fashions from Paris, but I keep my ears open in case I can learn something, not about the clothes but about the war.

All I hear are the same complaints I've heard at my house.

"Those murderin' Yankees . . ."

"That damned man, Mr. Lincoln, should be shot."

The women gasp; the men apologize for using bad language. Mrs. Hamilton stands and taps her glass with a spoon. "Ladies, I believe it's time to leave the gentlemen to their port and cigars," she says. "Come with me."

Finally, it's over and I can escape.

Pleading exhaustion, I flee to my room. It's the same one I always use when at the Hamiltons', and luckily it's plenty big enough for two people. There's a four-poster bed, a huge armoire, and a small table where I set down the treats—corn bread and a slice of lemon cake—that I've smuggled upstairs inside a napkin for Sam.

But where is she?

Someone—I hope it was Sam—has unpacked my trunk, and Theo's breeches are draped over a chair. A slip of paper sticks up from the side pocket. Curious, I pull it out:

Meet me at the barn, Sam.

My heart skips a beat. Should I go after her or just wait and hope she doesn't get into trouble? Behind me the door opens. Relieved, I whirl around so fast, I get dizzy.

"Sam . . . ?"

The word dies on my lips.

In a flash, Alice Hamilton is beside me. I had no idea she could move that quickly. She snatches the note from my hand.

"What's this?"

"Private," I snap. "Give it back."

Her eyebrows knit together like two fuzzy caterpillars. Then she gives an evil little laugh. "*You* have a beau, and you're meeting him in the barn."

"Am not," I say.

Alice smirks. "My mother won't approve."

Neither will mine.

But I can't admit that Sam is a girl and that she's my maid because it will raise a huge fuss. Slaves don't write; they don't leave messages in pockets, either. On the other hand, if I sigh and beg Alice to keep a secret—one girl to another—and pre-

tend that Sam is a young man I like, that will cause an even
bigger fuss.

Then Alice notices Theo's breeches. "What are *those*
doing here?"

"They're my brother's."

"Is he coming, too?" Alice says.

She flirted with him last Christmas, but he doesn't like her
any better than I do. "No," I say, thinking fast. "My maid is
new. She packed them by mistake, and—"

Inspiration strikes.

"That's an old note of Theo's," I say, snatching it back.
"From . . . from Samuel Wade."

"Who's he?" Alice says.

"Theo's best friend."

Not even close to the truth, but it's the first thing I can
think of. Sam Wade is the son of a tenant farmer and my
brother used to play with him when they were little. Last I
heard, Sam had joined the Confederate Army, but Alice
wouldn't know that.

Pouting, she says, "Mama says you're to come downstairs."

"Now?"

"I'm to give a piano recital."

This elevates my punishment to a whole other level. When
Alice plays the piano, it sounds as if a cat has gotten stuck between the foot pedals.

It's even worse when she sings.

Gathering up my skirts, I follow Alice and hope that
Samantha's keeping herself out of trouble.

17

SAMANTHA

Mississippi, July 1863

"NOBODY WILL CHALLENGE YOU," my brother always said, "if you behave as if you're supposed to be exactly where you are."

So I take his advice.

With my head up, I stride purposefully toward what I hope is the horse barn. It's hard to tell because there are sheds and small buildings all over the place. One looks like a blacksmith, but I'm only guessing based on the noise I hear from inside. I cross a small wooden bridge and look longingly at the stream that gurgles and splashes beneath it.

I'd love to jump in, clothes and all.

I've spent the last two hours unpacking Caroline's trunk and putting away her gowns, and I'm ready to melt. Tomorrow I might even wear that burlap skirt. It's got to be way cooler than this dress, never mind if the burlap itches worse than the seams on my underwear and cotton socks.

Smoke curls from the metal chimney of a low building on my left. I feel sorry for whoever's working in there—it must be really, really hot. Beyond it, I see a cluster of small cabins. Caroline said that's where the Hamiltons' slaves live.

A man chops wood; two women wearing brown dresses and straw hats jiggle babies on their hips. Children play in the dirt with sticks, watched over by slightly bigger children.

They're all barefoot.

I've managed to squash my feet into the boots that Pearl provided but they're already killing me. Quickly, I step to one side to avoid a groom leading a frisky black horse. Its nostrils flare and there's a chain over its nose.

A yearling colt, I'm guessing.

And there's the barn. It has to be, because I can smell it. It's different from the barns with pigs and chickens and cows that I've already passed. I step inside and inhale the familiar aroma of horses, fresh hay, and oiled leather.

For a moment, I pause.

Nothing has changed. It's just the same here as it is in my barn, one hundred fifty years from now. Horses whicker, buckets clank, and I can almost feel Nugget nuzzling my hands for a carrot. Across the aisle is a horse that looks just like him—golden chestnut with a blond mane and tail.

Do they call it blond here?

Flaxen?

I have no idea.

Could this horse be one of Nugget's ancestors? His stall's nameplate says *Spinner*, but I don't recognize it from Nugget's pedigree.

"Hi, Spinner," I say.

He flattens his ears and tries to nip my arm, but I can tell it's a big sham. He has a kind eye, and that's a good sign. Slowly, I hold out my hand so he can smell me.

"Careful, miss," says a voice behind me. "That gelding is hard to handle." He sounds like a white man, with an accent that's hard to place. Caroline has warned me about the Hamilton's overseer. She says he's meaner than a weasel.

Slowly, I turn, being careful to keep my head down so he can't see my eyes.

"Oh, you're a *slave*," he says and spits on the floor, narrowly missing the hem of my skirt. "Git on out of here."

In less than a second, I shift into judo mode—legs apart, knees bent, arms flexed and ready. It would be so easy to take him out and he'd never know what hit him, like the bullies at school. My black belt keeps them all at bay. But decking this man would be a disaster. With a deep breath, I pull myself together.

I am *not* at school.

I am in a nineteenth-century horse barn facing a man with a whip—a mean looking thing with a knotted leather thong—and I can tell he's dying to use it on me.

"Yes, mister," I mumble.

He raises the whip. "Go."

So I shuffle off trying to look as dejected as possible, but inside I am raging with fury. *How did my people live like this?*

But they did.

And this is what my mother has been trying to tell me and I've been doing my best to ignore. I've paid scant attention to Mom's lessons on emancipation, Rosa Parks, and the Civil Rights movement, figuring that we've all moved beyond it.

Yeah, yeah, Mom, I hear you.

I even blew off one of her Martin Luther King Day celebrations so I could ride with Jenna, and now I'm desperate to call Mom and apologize and tell her she was right.

But I've slammed into a time warp.

And it's ugly.

I hide in the shadows in case Caroline shows up, but she doesn't and now it's getting dark. Dinner would've been over an hour ago. I didn't have any, and my stomach is complaining. Lunch with Dad was in a different century. Right now, I'd love to order a pizza—sausage with peppers and extra cheese. I pull out my cell, just in case this is all a dream, but of course there's no service. I am well and truly stuck.

And now it's well and truly dark.

At the risk of running down my battery, I use my iPhone's flashlight to help find my way back. I don't need to be falling into that stream, even though it's still hot and I'd love to get wet—and cool. Then I remember what Theo said about cell phones gobbling up power when you turn them on and they search for a connection. Quickly, I switch my phone into airplane mode.

Yeah, right. As if there are airplanes here.

The paths are deserted, but faintly I hear singing. It's coming from the big house. Feeling like a spy, I creep closer and peek through a tall window. Women in enormous crinolines and men with starched collars and cutaway jackets stand around a grand piano like the one we have at home. That girl, Alice, is playing . . . badly, from what I can hear. Looking bored, Caroline sits beside her.

I guess she never found my note.

Cautiously, I climb the back stairs to our room. I don't dare use my flashlight in case I run into someone, so I rely on the oil lamps that sit on tables and hang on walls. I hate it that whales had to give their lives for this.

It's nine o'clock.

If I were at home, I'd be settling down with Mom and Dad to watch a movie, or I'd be texting with Jenna and *pretending* to watch a movie. There is nothing to do in this room. There are no books to read, nothing to see. It's darker than a tomb in here. It's also hot and airless. I fling up the window and a bazillion tiny bugs hit my face.

No screen.

So I shut the window.

The door opens. Holding a lantern, Caroline comes in. She locks the door and leans against it.

"Phew," I say. "I'm glad you're back."

"Me, too."

"Did you find my note?"

She nods, then reams me out. "You have to be more careful," she says, and I decide not to tell her how close I came to losing it in the Hamiltons' barn.

We help each other out of our dresses, then sit on the bed in our chemises. I guess this is what we'll sleep in, too. When I unpacked Caroline's trunk, I didn't see anything that resembled a nightgown . . . or bras.

I guess they haven't been invented yet.

Caroline fiddles with the ribbons on her bloomers. "What do you call these in Dutch?"

"Ribbons?"

"No, bloomers."

"I don't know," I say. "But knickers are *onderbroek*."

She tries to get her tongue around the word and makes such a hash of it, we both laugh. My Dutch is rusty, so we try for something easier and I give her all of Dad's stock phrases, including heels down: *Heilen omlaag*.

The battery on my iPhone is at seventy-five percent, which is pretty good, except I know that it drains a little every day even when it's turned off. But Caroline wants to see more, so I tell her about iTunes.

"It's like magic," she says, fingering her locket. Is she going to sleep in it?

"You got a boyfriend in there?" I say.

Caroline snaps it open. "Pandora."

"What a cool idea," I say, peering at the tiny photo. It's black and white and kind of fuzzy, but Pandora looks like a horse I would love to ride.

"I'm supposed to have Mama and Papa in here—until I get a husband," Caroline says, closing it again. "But I'd rather have a horse."

"Me, too."

"And music," she says.

So I click on a video of One Direction, my favorite group. Even Mom loves these guys because they've done an amazing job of raising money for kids in Africa, and in no time at all, Caroline's snapping her fingers and bobbing to the beat of "One Way or Another."

Then I teach her a couple of dance steps, and we collapse onto the bed, giggling. It's almost like being with Jenna except we'd be wearing tank tops and shorts and eating popcorn.

My stomach rumbles.

Caroline says, "Here, I brought these for you."

From the table, she picks up a napkin I hadn't noticed and unwraps it. I literally fall on the food. Corn bread has never tasted so good, and the lemon cake is gone in a flash.

"I would have brought more," Caroline says, as I wipe crumbs off my mouth, "but I didn't think you'd care for battered oysters." She rolls her eyes. "Besides, Alice ate them all."

I stick out my tongue, and we giggle all over again.

Which just goes to show . . .

If you're going to time travel back to the nineteenth century, don't land in Alice Hamilton's bed; land in Caroline Chandler's.

She's a lot more fun.

✢ 18 ✢

CAROLINE

Mississippi, July 1863

ON SUNDAY MORNING, Mrs. Hamilton insists that I accompany them to church, even though I fake a convincing headache.

"Praying will make it better," she says.

"I can do that here," I reply.

Her eyebrows shoot up as if she's never heard anyone— least of all a girl—argue with her before, and certainly not about attending church. For a moment, nobody moves until Alice lays a hand on my arm and pinches me so hard it hurts.

"Mama," she says. "Do we know a family called Wade?"

"No," says her mother. "Why do you ask?"

Alice gives a dramatic sigh. "They have a son named Samuel, and—"

Is she blackmailing me?

Come to church with us, or I'll tell Mama about the note?

I hold my breath, waiting for the worst, but Mr. Hamilton strides up. "The coach is ready," he says. I want to kiss his cheek and thank him for saving the day.

"Caroline, where's your bonnet?" says Mrs. Hamilton.

Her beady eyes, black as raisins, sweep over my dull red gown, and it only takes a moment for her to realize that I'm not wearing my crinoline. "Get your gloves," she says, sniffing. "You can't go out like this."

With no other option, I send Sam upstairs.

She's been hovering in the background, playing the part of devoted servant and hoping I wouldn't have to spend the morning in church. We'd planned a trip to the barn as soon as the Hamiltons and the overseer left in their carriage, but dear Alice has ruined everything.

If I refuse to attend church, she will tattle on me. I walk to the foot of the stairs and take my bonnet and gloves from Sam.

"Sorry," I whisper.

"Come along," says Mrs. Hamilton.

I cram on my bonnet and tie the ribbons, then struggle to pull the cotton gloves over my hands, now damp with perspiration. Sam has shown me photos of what girls in her century wear—no crinolines or bonnets or corsets. If I wasn't so fascinated, I'd be shocked. All that bare leg . . . and the bathing suits! I'm having a hard time with that one, but I'm sure Theo would love it.

I can't wait for him to meet Sam.

As I walk toward the carriage, Mr. Hamilton cups my elbow and invites me to accompany him on his afternoon ride. Poor man. His wife and daughter won't go anywhere near a horse, and his son, Joseph, has been away fighting for over a year. Nobody's heard from him since late April. They fear he was killed at Chancellorsville.

More than thirty thousand dead.

The South won that battle, but after meeting Sam and talking to Theo about the war, I'm more confused than ever. Somebody needs to stop the killing. So far I haven't dared to ask Sam who won. Of course she knows, but she hasn't said anything.

I think that means we lost.

The slaves don't go to church. It's not allowed. Theo says it's because the masters are afraid that if slaves learn to read the Bible they will find out that what we're doing to them is wrong.

I worry about my brother.

I'm scared he'll run away and join the North, and we'll never see him again.

Church takes forever. It always does. The minister drones on about how God has given the South a fresh and golden opportunity to realize a new form of government that addresses the just and constitutional rights of . . .

Whom? I find myself asking.

But the minister doesn't answer that question. He just keeps talking in circles until I'm half asleep. Every time I feel myself nodding off, Alice digs me in the ribs.

Finally, it's over.

Outside the church, Mr. and Mrs. Hamilton shake hands with other plantation owners while I keep my distance. Fluttering her skimpy eyelashes, Alice simpers over the neighbors' sons. Those boys will be off to war soon, but Alice doesn't understand. She still thinks that life is a never-ending round of balls and teas, of dashing young men who fill your dance card and chaperones who frown when those young men even think about kissing your hand.

"Chaperones?" Sam had said. "What are those?"

I'd tried to explain, but it was just another barrier—her world and mine. She could no more understand why we had chaperones than I could understand why she did not.

"Freedom," she'd said.

It's a word I'm still trying to understand.

Mr. Hamilton says, "If you'd care to ride with me this afternoon, be ready by two o'clock. You can have my favorite mare."

Her name is Skylark. She's dark bay and a half sister to Pandora—their dam is my father's mare, Nigella, which is why I like riding her. My father and Mr. Hamilton have been crossbreeding their horses since before I was born. Their interwoven pedigrees get more complicated every year. Even I have a hard time keeping track of them.

While a groom saddles Skylark, I visit Allegra—another of Pandora's half sisters—across the aisle and stroke her velvety brown nose. She belongs to my father and she's here to

be bred to Hyperion. She won't come home until they are sure
she is with foal.

"Your mare is ready," says Mr. Kelley, the overseer. He
leads Skylark from her stall and then hoists me into the awkward side saddle. His bony hands grip my waist so hard I
almost cry out.

"Thank you," I say and move off.

Mr. Hamilton mounts Hyperion, his chestnut stallion. But
as we're about to leave, the overseer leads Spinner outside,
vaults into the saddle, and follows Mr. Hamilton and me.

"Spinner needs the exercise," Mr. Hamilton explains as
we ride toward the cotton fields. "That horse is such a handful that we have to keep him busy."

"So why not turn him outside?"

That's what my father does with our horses. He lets them
run loose, but it seems as if Mr. Hamilton prefers to keep his
horses inside the barn.

"Because he jumps out," Mr. Hamilton says, sounding
proud. "There isn't a fence around here that can hold him."

Poor Spinner.

No wonder he's so restless, cooped up all day. I don't
think I've ever seen him with his ears forward, even now, out
riding. Then again, Mr. Kelley's spurs are enough to make
even the gentlest horse put its ears back.

We're halfway through our ride when the overseer canters
off to check a broken fence. Ten minutes later he returns and
says that Mr. Hamilton should take a look, too.

"Then you stay here with my guest," Mr. Hamilton says.

The overseer tips his hat. "It will be my pleasure."

But not mine. I don't trust this man.

The moment Mr. Hamilton disappears, Mr. Kelley pulls into place beside me, on my left and far too close. "You enjoying yourself, miss?" he says. One of his teeth is missing, and he spits when he talks.

"Yes, thank you."

"You must ride whenever you want," he goes on. "I'll be honored to go with you if Mr. Hamilton can't."

His knee brushes against mine, a most unpleasant sensation. I touch Skylark with my whip and pull away, but I can feel Mr. Kelley's narrow eyes following my every move.

When I catch up with Mr. Hamilton, I heave a sigh of relief. If I didn't have my own father, I would want him.

"You look a little pale," he says. "Are you all right?"

"I am well, thank you." I smile as best I can.

We enjoy the rest of our ride with the overseer trailing behind, but the minute we reach the barn I slide off Skylark, hand her reins to a groom, and rush off.

I hate doing that.

I should be rubbing that horse down, feeding her treats, and telling her how much I loved our time together. Instead, I race up to my room, close the door, and lean against it, breathing hard.

"Are you okay?" Sam says.

19

SAMANTHA

Mississippi, July 1863

"NO," CAROLINE SAYS.

"What happened?" I ask.

She tells me, and I want to slam that miserable overseer, hard. The sooner we're out of here, the better. But we have another four days to go . . . unless, of course, I figure out a way to go back home.

So far, nobody's remarked on my blue eyes, probably because I've kept my head down and most of the time I'm with Caroline. She's a guest, so the other slaves aren't about to ask questions—not in public, anyway. Whatever they might be saying, they're keeping it to themselves, far from the ears of their owners.

"Did you have anything to eat?" Caroline says.

I pull a face. "Yes."

I ate lunch in the slaves' kitchen and almost threw up. Corn mush and salted herring. I'm not crazy about fish but I was hungry enough to eat it, just like the others did.

Even the kids.

I looked at their adorable faces and wondered how they'd feel about pizza, hot dogs, or an ice-cream sundae. The little girl sitting next to me tucked her hand into mine. I squeezed it gently and was rewarded with a gap-toothed grin. I tell Caroline it's time the Tooth Fairy paid a visit.

"You can't," she says.

"Why not?"

"Because you have nothing to give her."

I glance around this lavish room filled with silver hairbrushes, ivory combs, and enough old furniture to make antique dealers swoon. Would anyone miss that wooden bead I found on the floor or the pearl button that fell off Caroline's dress this morning? If I still had that dime, I'd give it to her. I pick up a tiny candle, almost worn to a stub.

"How about this?"

"She'll be punished," Caroline says.

I stare at her. "You have got to be kidding."

"For stealing."

Bit by bit, it's sinking in.

The next three days go by in a blur, filled with afternoon teas, music recitals, and endless poetry readings that would drive even my mother insane. Keeping my head down, I follow Caroline around and count the hours until we can leave the Hamiltons' plantation.

But there's one thing I will miss.

Running water.

Yes, they actually have it here. And of course I'm not supposed to use it, being a slave, so naturally I did. Yesterday, Caroline stood guard outside the bathroom—or whatever they call it now—and she even found something that resembled a bar of soap. The water was cold, but I didn't care, and I now feel clean for the first time since I fell asleep in that four-poster bed on Friday afternoon.

Dad must be tearing his hair out.

Mom, too.

I make a vow that I will never argue with her again.

Ever.

That night I discuss it with Caroline. She's borrowed a book from Mr. Hamilton's library about the South's decision to secede. Its language is old-fashioned and impenetrable, but I manage to pull out a few passages that make sense—that is, if you agree with secession.

I am so out of my depth here.

But my mother would be all over it. So I try to dredge up all she's taught me. It's there, somewhere, squirreled away in my brain. Bit by bit, it comes out, and I end up arguing with Caroline about race and politics. She bursts into tears when I tell her that the North won.

"President Lincoln was shot," I say.

She gasps.

How much, really, can you share? It's one thing to talk

about music and dancing and horses, but wars and dead presidents are something else again. I think I'll wait a bit before telling her that we now have a black president. Caroline's come a long way since I suddenly showed up in her bed, but I don't think she's quite ready for Barack Obama.

Yet.

Tomorrow, maybe.

That's when we'll return to the Chandlers' plantation. Caroline wants me to meet Theo—properly this time, as a friend. Somehow, she promises, we will all ride together, but I don't see how she's going to pull it off.

Maybe I won't have to.

Maybe I'll have figured out a way to get home by then.

I'm helping Caroline pack her trunk when I hear voices outside below our bedroom window. Parting the curtains, I look down. Alice's father stands in the driveway talking to a couple of soldiers. They wear bedraggled gray uniforms, and they look half starved. So do their horses. I wave Caroline over.

She gasps. "That's Sam Wade."

"Who?"

"He's the boy I said was Theo's friend, remember? When Alice read your note about meeting me in the barn?"

"Oh, right."

"I'd better go down," she says. "You stay here and keep an eye out for Alice. She's probably still in bed, but if she comes downstairs and someone introduces her to Sam Wade, she'll—"

Turning on a Dime

"Put two and two together and come up with five?"

Caroline rolls her eyes. "I won't even try to sort that out," she says, then heads for the door. Her blue gown—almost the same shade as mine—sweeps across the floor like a giant broom.

"Wait up," I say.

She turns. "What?"

"This." I fasten the top buttons on the back of her dress.

"Thanks," she says. "I don't know what I'd do without you."

I'm beginning to wonder the same thing about her. What will it be like when I finally figure out how to get back home and Caroline isn't with me?

❧ 20 ❧

CAROLINE

Mississippi, July 1863

WHEN I REACH THE FRONT PORCH, I see no sign of Alice or her mother—just Mr. Hamilton and the two soldiers. I hardly recognize Sam Wade. The last time I saw him, he had plump cheeks and a generous waistline. Right now, he resembles one of his father's scrawny cows. None of the men seem to notice my arrival.

I hide behind a column and listen.

Mr. Hamilton says, "You mean to say those Yankees just took over the house?"

"Yessir," Sam Wade replies. "Saw them do it myself."

"What happened to the family?"

"They took off around dawn on a buckboard."

"Did you talk to them?" Mr. Hamilton says. "Find out where they were heading?"

"Didn't get a chance," Sam Wade says. "Not with all them Union soldiers running around." He pats his uniform and clouds of dust waft out. "We had to stay out of sight."

"Did they all get away?"

Sam Wade takes off his hat and scratches his head. It's probably full of lice. "I don't know," he says. "There were only two men and two ladies on that buckboard, but I could swear Mister Theo had another sister."

Theo?

Is he talking about my family?

My house?

Without thinking twice, I abandon my hiding place and rush down the marble steps so fast I almost fall over. Mr. Hamilton puts his arm around my shoulders and I lean into him, shaking.

"I'm sure that your family is perfectly fine, my dear," he says, patting my shoulder as if I were a nervous horse. "This is just a misunderstanding, that's all."

"No, it's not," I say. "I heard what you said."

Swallowing hard, I turn toward Sam Wade who's now blushing redder than one of his father's tomatoes. I can still remember how delicious they tasted. "Sam, you recognize me, don't you?"

"Yes, ma'am," he says.

"So, tell me."

He looks down at his feet. "Miz Caroline, I—"

His companion cuts in. "Them Yankee soldiers have taken over the Chandler plantation. Sam and me . . . we watched from a hill behind the barn. I'm sorry, miss, but we was outnumbered. We couldn't have stopped them."

I pause for a minute, taking this all in. "What about the rest of your men?" Surely they could fend off a bunch of Yankees.

The soldier looks at Sam, then at Mr. Hamilton, and finally at me. "They ran away," he says.

No wonder we lost the war.

"What about my family?" I say, feeling sick. "Where have they gone? What's happened to them?"

"No telling, Miz Caroline," Sam says. "Most people go south or east when driven from their homes." He pauses to scratch his head again, and I shudder to think of what his finger nails are finding.

The other soldier takes over. "They can't go west because of the river," he says. "So maybe they're heading for Louisiana. Do you have kinfolk there?"

The only one is Aunt Maude.

But she's in New Orleans, and the Yankees own it. Their armies occupy the city, although my aunt wrote to my mother three months ago and said that she and her family were doing very well. They live on a large plantation far enough away from the city and provide supplies for the Union troops.

She is probably getting rich off this.

If only we could tap into the amazing information that Sam says is on her iPhone. I still trip over that word and others that sound really strange to my ears—Facebook and Google and Twitter. With them I could find out where my parents are and if they're safe.

But none of it exists yet.

I almost wish I hadn't met Sam, because then I wouldn't know what is possible and what the future holds.

"How far is New Orleans?" I say.

"One hundred and twenty miles as the crow flies," Mr. Hamilton says. "About seven days' journey on a buckboard."

"Then I will go to them," I say, having no idea how I'm to accomplish this. I pull free from Mr. Hamilton's arms.

"Don't be foolish, child," he says. "You will remain with us."

Sam Wade clears his throat. "You'd best move away, sir," he says. "Them Yankees are murderin' thieves. They're looting and stealing horses."

Theo's words.

"My father's beautiful horses," I say, still looking at Sam Wade. "Which ones did he take?"

"Couldn't rightly say, Miz Caroline. It was still pretty dark, but far as I could see, he hitched up that buckboard to a couple of mares."

"Black?"

"I think so."

That would be Celeste and Nigella because they're the best we have for harness work. "Was my father riding a black stallion?" I ask, unable to imagine Papa leaving Raven behind.

Sam Wade shakes his head. "Just those two mares. I reckon that's all the soldiers allowed him to take. They'll be wanting the stallions and geldings for their own use."

This means that Pandora is safe.

For now, anyway.

An upstairs window opens and Mrs. Hamilton looks out. "Edward, what's going on?"

Her husband glances up. "Mary, come down and take Caroline inside. She's just had some bad news."

—————◌∞◌—————

Heeding Sam Wade's advice, Mr. Hamilton declares that it's no longer safe for them to remain at home with Union soldiers so close to hand. He tells his wife to start packing.

Boxes and trunks pile up in the foyer.

Servants scurry back and forth with baskets of food; the house hums with rumors. I overhear the housekeeper telling Mrs. Hamilton that she's heard talk of General Grant himself riding up to the house tomorrow morning and claiming it for his men.

"Nonsense," says Mrs. Hamilton. Her face is flushed bright pink. She's not accustomed to physical exercise.

Neither is Alice.

Between bouts of crying, she wanders around in a daze, getting in everyone's way. Her father finally tells her to go and lie down. Then he directs his grooms to prepare the carriage and two wagons for their journey. They will leave at dawn and travel with the overseer and three slaves to the home of Mr. Hamilton's brother in Biloxi. The situation there is more stable, he assures his frightened family. He orders me to go with them.

"I'm going home," I say.

"That, my dear," Mr. Hamilton says kindly, "is out of the question. Now run along and make yourself useful. I'm sure my wife would appreciate help with the packing." He pauses. "And, please, would you see if Alice is all right?"

Reluctantly, I climb the stairs and knock on Alice's door. She's curled beneath a quilt on her bed, facing away from the door. It clicks shut behind me and Alice turns around.

"Oh, it's you."

Her face is blotchy; her eyes red from crying. She's also shivering, despite the heat. "Can I get you anything?" I say. "A glass of water? Another quilt?"

Alice says, "Will the Yankees steal my home as well?"

"Of course not," I say, with more confidence than I feel. "They've already got mine. They won't need another."

This is the kind of thing Sam would say.

Sam?

In all the chaos, I'd forgotten about her. She has no idea what's going on—not since I raced downstairs, determined to keep Sam Wade from talking to Alice.

As if that matters any more.

❧ 21 ❧

SAMANTHA

Mississippi, July 1863

CAROLINE CHARGES THROUGH THE DOOR like a runaway horse. I've finally managed to stuff everything into her trunk—I could swear her clothes have doubled in size—and have closed the lid.

"Hey, hold on," I say.

She stops, breathing hard. "I won't go."

"Where to?"

"Biloxi," she says.

My knowledge of geography is even sketchier than my knowledge of history. "Where's that?"

"South," Caroline says, waving toward a window that faces east. I know this because the sun wakes me up every morning.

"Sit." I point to the bed.

She doesn't argue, and we sit side-by-side—a black girl and a Southern belle—holding hands on a four-poster bed that I shouldn't even be sitting on. "Tell me what happened."

When Caroline's all cried out, I give her a hug, because that's what you do when friends are hurting. She stiffens for a moment, then relaxes and leans against me like a rag doll.

"I'm sorry about your family," I say.

Caroline wipes her eyes. "Thank you."

"So, where's Biloxi?" I ask again.

On the Gulf Coast, I find out. I also find out that I definitely don't want to go there. It might be a really cool place with beaches and a boardwalk, but it's further away from here than her house is—like hundreds of miles further. I'd never be able to get back to the twenty-first century from Biloxi, even if I could figure out how to do it.

"We have to go home," Caroline says.

I nod. "Okay, but when?"

"Tonight," she says. "After dark."

"How?" I say.

There are no street lights out there, no maps or GPS to guide us. I don't even know which direction the Chandlers' plantation is. I paid no attention when we drove here. I was too busy worrying about the horses' check reins and not blowing my cover with the driver.

Caroline bites her lip. "We'll sneak into the barn, borrow a couple of horses, and by dawn we'll be back at my house."

"And after that?" I say.

"We swap horses and ride south to catch up with my

family. They won't be going fast with a buckboard. We'll—"
Caroline gives me a defiant look as if I'm going to argue with
her plan.

And I probably will because it's full of holes, but I'd like
to hear the rest of the plan. Not that I have a better one, other
than finding the magic genie that got me into this mess in the
first place.

"We'll take Pandora and Raven," she goes on. "My father
will be pleased to have his stallion back."

"Raven?" I ask.

She nods. "He's Pandora's sire.

"Okay," I say. "But you're forgetting one thing."

"What?"

"The soldiers."

She gives a little shudder, and I know that I've hit a home
run. Caroline is worried about those Union guys, and I can't
blame her. Soldiers are wicked tough because they have to be.
I've watched the news on TV from the Middle East and
Afghanistan.

"I know what to do," Caroline says.

I raise my eyebrows. "Okay, shoot."

"I'll find the chief soldier, and—"

"The general," I prompt.

Caroline nods. "Yes, I'll find the general, and I'll tell him
that the North wins the war, so they may as well stop fighting
right now." She catches her breath. "It would save thousands
of lives."

I can't argue with that. "But—"

She looks at me. "What?"

"I don't think you can alter events, because if you do, it messes up the future, and—"

"So?"

"Think about it," I say. "Suppose I found one of my ancestors here—my great-great-whatever-grandfather when he was still a boy—and I killed him."

She gasps. "That's murder."

"It's hypothetical," I say. "If I killed my great-something-grandfather, then I would not exist."

It takes a moment for my words to sink in, not only into her head but into mine as well. This is all so confusing that I don't know where to begin figuring it out. Erik would know, of course. Trouble is, his explanations of time travel fell on my deaf ears in much the same way that my mother's history lessons did. Caroline finds her voice first.

"So there's nothing we can do?"

"Yes, there is."

"What?"

"We can calm down and take it one step at a time," I say. "First, we have to get out of here. So let's concentrate on that, okay?"

Caroline nods. "Okay."

I give her a high five—something else she's learned—because we both have the same agenda. We want to get back home, except that for us, home is two totally different places.

Afternoon tea is eaten on the run. Even Mrs. Hamilton rushes about with a piece of seed cake in her hand as she directs her servants. There are so many baskets and trunks in the foyer that I can't imagine them all fitting into a couple of buckboards.

Caroline has already found out which horses they're taking. Mr. Hamilton will ride Hyperion, the overseer will ride Skylark, and they will put six horses in harness—two for each vehicle.

Spinner, it turns out, is staying behind.

So is Allegra, because she belongs to Caroline's father. I guess Mr. Hamilton doesn't care about them, any more than he cares about the slaves he is leaving to the mercies of the Union Army. I cross my fingers and hope the slaves will be freed.

"Okay," I say. "Then let's ride Allegra and Spinner to your house."

"You want to ride *him*?" Caroline says.

"Why not?"

"He's a beast."

"Only with the overseer."

I've already figured that out. Yesterday I slipped into the barn again when nobody was around, and Spinner didn't pin his ears once. He loved the apple core I fed him that I'd pinched from the kitchen.

We can take nothing with us, but Caroline doesn't care. "I hate all these clothes," she says, glaring at her trunk. It's supposed to be downstairs with the others, but it will stay in the Hamilton's guest room, gathering dust until they return.

Or not.

We've already planned our escape clothes. I'm to wear my

tank top and Theo's breeches beneath my white blouse and burlap skirt, while Caroline will wear her riding habit. She managed to steal food from one of the baskets—half a meat pie, corn bread, and two peaches—that we've stuffed into a pillowcase and will take turns carrying.

Caroline has also found a map.

Well, sort of. It's a rough sketch of the Hamiltons' land showing the big house and its outbuildings, one main road, a network of winding paths, the cotton fields, and an outer perimeter line with a tiny arrow that I assume is pointing north. Caroline also found out that her plantation lies due west of here. Shortly before dusk, we're going outside to watch where the sun is setting and figure out some landmarks to head for, like tall trees. It'd be great if they had cell towers and telephone poles as well, but—

Then, after dark when everyone's gone to bed, Caroline and I will grab our horses and leave.

At least, that's the plan.

22

CAROLINE

Mississippi, July 1863

WHILE PRETENDING THAT I'M GOING to Biloxi with the Hamiltons, I do my best to help. I count silverware and table linen, making sure the right number of knives, forks, spoons, and napkins are packed into each crate, although why Mrs. Hamilton thinks she needs all this paraphernalia is a mystery. She's fleeing for her life—not giving a dinner party.

"I'm afraid we don't have enough room to bring your maid," Mr. Hamilton says. "But when we return from Biloxi and your family is settled back home, we will send her to you."

"Thank you," I say.

Because really, what else can I do?

Mr. Hamilton has no idea that Sam and I will be racing off after dark on a couple of his horses. Well, only one, because Allegra belongs to my father. I want to tell Mr. Hamilton that I'll send Spinner home as soon as he, Mr. Hamilton, sends Sam back to me. Hypothetically, that is.

Sam would laugh over this.

Finally, things begin to slow down. Alice remains in her room, the exhausted servants retreat to their cabins, and Mrs. Hamilton hauls herself up the stairs hanging onto the banister like she was ninety-two rather than forty-two—only three years older than my mother.

Where is Mama right now?

I feel guilty about not kissing her good-bye, but she'd been more concerned over my lack of bonnet and gloves than over my departure. I try to picture my mother on a buckboard, bouncing its way south toward New Orleans.

Father will manage and so will Theo, but Louise won't and neither will my mother. They will be fussing over their clothes and complaining about the dust, and—

All of a sudden it's six o'clock.

I give Mr. Hamilton a spontaneous hug because I don't have any idea when—or even if—I will ever see him again, and I leave him looking a little surprised as I race up the stairs. I pass Joseph's old room and stop. Someone, a maid probably, has packed shoes and boots into a crate and left it in a corner. On top is a pair of boots that I think will fit Sam quite nicely.

I glance around to make sure I'm alone.

Then I grab the boots and run down the hall much faster

than a young lady should and burst through the bedroom door.

"Here," I say, tossing the boots at Sam.

"Wow, these are cool," she says, slipping her bare feet into them.

"Do they fit?"

"Perfectly," Sam says. "And I won't ask where you found them." She's already wearing her traveling clothes, so I climb into mine.

We're almost ready to go.

Sam walks to the window and parts the curtains. "Change of plans."

"What?"

"We'll go outside to check the sun, and then we'll stay out. We can hide behind the barn till it's dark enough to leave."

"We're not coming back inside, then?"

She shakes her head. "Too risky."

"Okay," I say.

Instead of a high five, Sam gives me a thumbs-up. This crazy sign language is beginning to grow on me.

The air is heavy with heat as Sam and I creep down the back stairs and head for the barn. It's still very light, not even close to dusk. We'll have hours to wait before we can leave.

Sam puts a hand on my arm.

We stop while she consults the map, then points toward a tree that stands taller than the rest. It's on the crest of a far hill; behind it, the setting sun is a giant orb of butter melting into a sky shot with mauve, pink, and pewter that no painter would ever dare to copy. If I wasn't so nervous, I'd be able to appreciate it.

"That one," Sam says. "That's our compass."

How we're going to see it in the dark, I have no idea, but it's good to have something solid to aim for. Sam thinks we'll have a full moon tonight, so that will help—a lot.

I look around, half expecting Mr. Hamilton or his servant to come racing from the house to ask why we're out here, but the place is deserted . . . well, except for a couple of little kids playing stickball. One of them giggles.

"Sshh," Sam says.

We're a few yards from the barn when a man comes out leading a dark bay horse. It's one of Mr. Hamilton's harness horses that he's going to hitch up tomorrow.

"Coming through," the man says.

Mr. Kelley?

A tiny shape darts in front of the horse, and—

Sam is there.

Before my startled eyes, she scoops the child into her arms and rolls out of danger. Mr. Kelley raises his whip. It slashes down inches from Sam and the child.

"*You,*" Mr. Kelley snarls.

He's not looking at me; he's looking at Sam.

She scrambles to her feet, still holding the child. A little girl. I see a flash of white teeth with a gap in front. Sam thrusts her at me. I clutch hold of squirming arms and legs.

Crack!

Mr. Kelley's whip shatters the silence.

The horse yanks itself free and races back into the barn.

"Out of my way, miss," Mr. Kelley yells at me.

He's aiming for Sam.

She circles him like a panther, and I stand, rooted to the spot. I can't take my eyes off her. Is she completely crazy?

"Sam, *no!*" I cry.

The little girl clings to my neck. "What's your name?" I whisper.

"Hope."

Her breath is sweet and hot. It comes in quick gasps, just like mine. A second passes, then another, and now I'm not even sure I'm breathing at all.

23

SAMANTHA

Mississippi, July 1863

THIS TIME, I'M READY. *Really ready.* You don't run over a kid and expect me to let you get away with it. Slowly, the overseer coils his whip and prepares to strike.

My only decision is how badly to hurt him.

It's not just the judo. Dad has also taught me how to use my hands to apply the right amount of pressure after I've already brought an attacker to his knees. Maybe I'll be really cool and do the Vulcan nerve pinch like Mr. Spock does on *Star Trek.*

Up comes the whip.

Even faster, up comes my hand. I snatch the whip from Mr. Kelley, knee him in the groin, and flip him backward so fast his eyeballs spin.

It's over in a flash—him on the ground, me standing above him. I want to dig my heel into his chest like a warrior who's just slain a fire-breathing dragon. Yeah, it was dirty judo, using my knee like that, but it worked.

Caroline gasps.

"Get a rope," I say. Duct tape would be better, but I don't think it's been invented yet, like bras.

"Why?"

"Because I'm going to tie him up."

Already, the overseer is coming back to life. I apply a little pressure to his neck, and he goes limp again.

It's Erik's fault.

He's the one who made me watch all those *Star Trek* reruns, over and over until my eyes crossed. I never thought this crazy maneuver would work, but it has. Or else Mr. Kelley is a *Star Trek* fan and has decided to play along.

Yeah, right.

Small hands give me a length of rope.

"Thanks, Hope."

Her eyes are bigger than saucers. Caroline stands behind her, and Caroline's eyes are bigger than saucers, too. I wrap the rope around Mr. Kelley's wrists and knot it really tight.

"More rope," I say, "for his ankles."

Hope scuttles back into the barn and returns with tangle of rope that takes me a few precious minutes to sort out. After I tie Mr. Kelley's ankles together, Caroline helps me drag him inside. We heft him into an empty stall and half cover him with straw.

"What happens when he wakes up?" Caroline says.

"He'll have a very big headache."

"No," she says, sounding nervous. "I mean what happens when he tells people what you did?"

"He won't."

"Why not?"

"Think about it," I say, lifting Hope into my arms. "Do you really believe this guy is going to tell people that a black girl decked him?"

"No," Caroline says. "Because he won't call you a black girl, he'll call you a—"

"Hush," I say, hugging Hope.

She snuggles into my shoulder, and I wish I had that little wooden bead to give her. But I don't. So I kiss her warm cheek, wipe away her tears, and tell her to run really fast and find her mama. "Don't tell anyone about this," I whisper, "until the sun is high in the sky tomorrow, okay?"

Looking solemn, she nods. "Okay."

"See?" I say to Caroline. "Hope understands me."

I give Hope another kiss and scoot her out of the barn. I'm still trembling over what just happened. I don't enjoy hurting people, but Mr. Kelley deserved it. I strip off my burlap skirt.

I won't be needing that any more.

"So what will he say?" Caroline asks, staring at Mr. Kelley, now looking very peaceful amid a pile of clean straw.

"He'll blame the Union soldiers," I say. "He'll claim they snuck up on him, knocked him out and tied him up, and then—"

But Caroline worries about Hope, and I tell her not to.

There'll be chaos in the morning, and Mr. Kelley will be long gone with the Hamiltons before Hope tells her mother what really happened. There's no way he'll be able to take it out on them.

"But what if somebody finds him and he comes after us?" Caroline says.

"That's why we're going to leave, right now."

"But it's still light."

"We don't have a choice."

I close the stall door and slide its heavy bolts into place. It won't prevent Mr. Kelley from getting out—assuming he undoes the rope—but it'll slow him down.

Caroline hands me a bridle. "For Spinner."

Carefully, I approach him, but he doesn't pin his ears. I guess he's hoping for another treat. "Sorry, boy. Not this time," I say, slipping the bit into his mouth. That's when I remember our food.

"Do you have the pillowcase?"

"No. I thought you did."

We left in such a hurry, it's no wonder we both forgot. For a few mad moments I'm tempted to sneak back into the house, but someone would be bound to catch me. We were lucky to get away the first time without being seen.

"I guess we'll have to go hungry," I say.

Caroline leads Allegra into the aisle. "There'll be plenty of food at my house," she says, "unless the Yankees have eaten it all."

We take our horses outside. Their hooves clatter on the stones and I cringe, waiting for someone to yell at us. But all is quiet. Even though the sun is still out, the moon is rising in the east, playing hide and seek with clouds shaped like lambs' tails.

After giving Caroline a leg-up, I vault onto Spinner. We're riding bareback because Caroline doesn't want to be accused of stealing saddles.

"Just of stealing horses?" I say.

"Allegra belongs to my father."

"What about Spinner?"

She has no answer for that, and I'm glad, because riding him is exactly like riding Nugget.

Spinner dances along the main road, convinced that every rock and tree stump has huge teeth and claws waiting to pounce on him. It reminds me of riding Nugget when he hasn't been exercised in a few days.

Allegra's a lot calmer.

Maybe we should've stolen Skylark instead of Spinner. But Caroline reminds me that Mr. Hamilton wouldn't be as angry at losing Spinner as he would over losing Skylark because she's a mare and can be bred. Spinner's a gelding. He's of no use on a breeding farm except to carry the overseer around . . . and to help us get away.

"Hey, guess what?" I say.

Caroline pulls alongside me. "You want to play a guessing game?"

"Yes, because it'll help pass the time." I pause for dramatic effect. "Okay, so what two things are horses afraid of?"

"Only two?" she says. "I can think of hundreds."

I wait a couple of moments, but only to draw out the suspense. Not that we don't have enough of it already. I'm not sure, but I think we're being followed because I can hear hoof beats that aren't ours and something that sounds like a wheel grinding slowly over ruts and stones.

Slave catchers?

In the Hamiltons' kitchen I heard rumors and whispered stories about them—the bounty hunters who travel at night and capture fugitive slaves, then return them to their owners for a large reward. There would usually be three men—two on horseback and one driving a wagon to carry the slaves. But it's too early for the slave catchers to be out. It's probably an itinerant farmer and his family looking for a better life.

"I give up," Caroline says.

"Horses are afraid of only two things," I say. "Things that move and things that don't."

Caroline giggles.

For a few silly moments, we forget we're on the run. We bend over laughing even though this joke has been around for years. I heard it on Facebook and then Twitter, and then I realize that Caroline's hearing it for the first time.

She cocks her head. "Do you hear that?"

So, it's not my imagination . . . and they're getting closer.

"I'm scared," Caroline says.

I hate to admit it, but now I'm scared, too. How on earth can we ride to New Orleans if we can't even manage a few miles on private land? At least, I assume we're still on the Hamiltons' land. That tree we're keeping our eyes on never seems to get any nearer. So far, we've kept up a steady trot. Maybe it's time to canter.

"Listen," Caroline says.

Sure enough, whoever it is behind us is closing the gap. We need to hide, and we need to do it now.

"There," I say, pointing. "Follow me."

Taking the lead, I pull Spinner to the right, onto a path that looks barely wide enough for a rabbit. The woods aren't dense like they are at home, but they'll hide us well enough. Low hanging twigs snatch at my hair; brambles brush against my legs. A cart can't possibly follow us in here.

We've gone about a hundred yards, and I figure we're well out of sight when Caroline tells me to stop.

"Be quiet," she says.

On the main road, the sound of hooves and wheels draws closer. I hear men's voices—rowdy, drunken voices—and they're singing. I hold my breath as they rumble past and start to grow distant again.

"Phew," I say. "That was a close one."

"Yes," Caroline says. "But suppose they stop a bit further on, and we have to ride past them."

"We won't," I say. "As long as we keep on going."

Dropping the reins, I allow Spinner to graze. Eagerly, he snatches at whatever he finds on the ground as if nobody has ever let him do this before. I pull Caroline's crumpled map from my pocket.

"On this path?" she says.

"Yes."

If it's the one I think we're on, it's a shortcut that bypasses a huge loop in the main road that I vaguely remember from our journey last Saturday. If I'd known Caroline and I would be retracing our steps like this, I'd have paid more attention. Dusk is beginning to fall; the moon shines brightly through a lacework of branches. Gently, I pull Spinner's head up.

Something swoops toward us.

Whoo, whoot.

"Watch out!" I cry and duck.

Spinner erupts. He turns on a dime the way Nugget does and blunders into Allegra. She stumbles and goes down but rights herself almost immediately. Somehow, Caroline manages to stay on Allegra's back.

Grabbing a fistful of Spinner's mane, I manage to hang on while he snorts and tries to turn himself inside-out. Maybe this path isn't such a good idea after all.

"An owl," Caroline says.

I feel silly for panicking. "Yeah."

"There'll be bats, too," she whispers.

Oh, great.

All we need is a witch and a couple of cats, and we'll be ready for Halloween.

Or worse . . .

Mr. Kelley getting loose and coming after us.

24

CAROLINE

Mississippi, July 1863

WE PLUNGE DEEPER INTO THE WOODS. I hope Sam knows where we're going because I certainly don't. Her iPhone light flickers on and off as she checks the map.

I have no idea if it's even correct.

I found it in Mr. Hamilton's library when I went to fetch a book of poetry for Mrs. Hamilton that she'd decided she could not live without. The map fell from between its pages, and I now have visions of Alice's mother in the carriage reading Lord Tennyson to her family as they travel south. Thinking about silly things like this helps keep my mind off the things I ought to be thinking about, like—

Abruptly, Sam stops.

Allegra almost crashes into Spinner's rump, but he doesn't

kick out or even lift a hoof. He's a different horse with Sam on his back. I think she's bewitched him.

"What's wrong?" I say.

"I don't know," Sam says.

"So why did you—?"

Then I hear it. A mournful cry that sends a shiver down my spine. Twigs snap underfoot as Allegra skitters sideways. She must've heard it, too. I pat her neck. "It's all right, girl."

"Do you have wolves here?" Sam says.

"No."

"Coyotes?"

"I don't think so. At least, I've never heard of any in this part of Mississippi." Sam waves me forward. There's another wail, softer this time, almost like a whimper.

"It sounds like a dog," Sam says.

I let out my breath. "It's probably a hound."

My father's overseer keeps hounds. He uses them for hunting deer and possum and rounding up runaway slaves. I think about my maid, Ruth, and hope she got away. She was only sixteen—a year older than I am—and I can't begin to imagine what it must be like, running away in the middle of the night.

Oh, yes, I can. I'm doing it right now.

"I think it's hurt," Sam says.

"Who?"

"The dog." She kicks Spinner into a trot and I have no option but to follow, because there's no way I can hold Allegra back.

———— ∞ ————

Sam sees it first. She jumps off Spinner, hands his reins to me, and shoves her way into the undergrowth. The moon is so bright that I can see it twinkling off the blackberries that I'm tempted to snatch up and eat.

At least, I *think* they're blackberries.

Or they might be something poisonous, like pokeweed which needs to be cooked three times before you can eat it. Even then, it's likely to give you a stomach ache. Sam emerges from a tangle of vines with a puppy in her arms.

"He's hurt," she says.

"Where?"

"His paw, I think."

Still cradling the puppy, Sam drops to her knees. I get off Allegra and take the iPhone from her. I swipe my finger across the screen the way Sam showed me and tap the flashlight icon.

I shine it onto the puppy.

He can't be any older than four months, but he's nothing like the hounds that belong to my father's overseer, Zeke Turner. This dog has a thick, silvery coat and perky ears, and he looks just like a wolf. Gently, Sam examines his paw. He doesn't even object. He just lies in her arms as if he's happy to be there.

Definitely not a wolf.

"I think it's a thorn," Sam says.

A drop of blood oozes from the puppy's paw. I shine the light closer. With the tips of her fingers, Sam grips something I can't see and pulls it out. The puppy squeals.

"All better now," Sam says, as the puppy licks her hand. His tongue reaches for her face, and Sam laughs.

"What *is* he?" I say.

"Besides being cute?"

"Yes."

"He's a keeshond," Sam says.

"*Hound*?" I say. "He looks nothing like any hound I've ever seen."

"*Hond* is the Dutch word for 'dog'," Sam says, hugging the puppy as if he's a link to her other world. "I used to have one, and they're the sweetest, smartest dogs in the world." She drops a kiss on the puppy's nose. "They're also called Dutch Barge Dogs."

I've seen barges on the Mississippi River, but I doubt they're anything like the canal barges in Holland. "Why would you have a dog on a barge?"

"To catch the rats."

Behind me, something rustles and I almost jump out of my skin. I can tolerate snakes and mice and even spiders—but not rats. Theo had a pet rat once that he kept in a cage in his room. I used to have nightmares about it getting loose.

"I wonder who he belongs to," I say.

It must be somebody new because nobody around here has a dog like this. They've all got hounds, like our overseer. He's even nastier than Mr. Kelley, and I'm hoping he's also heading south with my family. But Sam Wade said that there were only two men on the buckboard. So which one got left behind? My brother or the overseer?

"Time to go," Sam says.

Snapping out of my thoughts, I give Sam her phone. She shoves it into her pocket, then gives me a leg-up onto Allegra and vaults onto Spinner's back as easily as if she were mounting a wooden rocking horse. The puppy looks up at her like he wants to ride on Spinner, too.

"Can he walk?" I say.

"Let's see," Sam says.

She urges Spinner along the trail. Favoring its paw, the puppy limps along beside her, looking determined to keep up. I think we just inherited a dog.

"What shall we call him?" I say.

Sam looks over her shoulder. "Fergus."

25

SAMANTHA

Mississippi, July 1863

MEMORIES OF MY OLD DOG push everything else from my mind, including the worry that we've just lost twenty minutes and are likely to run into trouble when we emerge from this trail. Fergus was Nugget's best friend—a horse and his dog.

They were inseparable.

Fergus came on trail rides with us, and he watched every lesson from the center of the ring, standing at my father's side and giving me critical looks, as if he'd memorized the dressage test and knew exactly what parts I needed to work on. He even preferred sleeping in Nugget's stall rather than in my bedroom. When Fergus was run over on Christmas Eve three years ago, I don't know who cried harder—me or Nugget.

We clung to each other like two survivors in a lifeboat. Yeah, I know we shouldn't ascribe human feelings to animals, but that's crazy. They make connections and best friends the way we do; and when one of those connections goes missing, they grieve.

I wipe my eyes.

And then I yawn. It's been a long day, and I'd give anything for a bed. But we have to keep going. You can't just decide to take a nap when you have a horse to take care of.

And a puppy.

How did I get myself into this mess? What oddball combination of events landed me in Mississippi in the middle of the Civil War? It's not as if I ever had a huge interest in the subject, much as my mother wished otherwise.

Now Erik, I could understand.

My brother would get a huge kick out of being whisked off to medieval England or outer space, and he'd be just as happy jousting with Sir Galahad as he would flying an X-wing like Luke Skywalker did. I just want to go home. I want my family, my horse, and—

I also want Caroline.

I can't imagine leaving her behind. She's become my best friend, like Jenna . . . like Fergus and Nugget. But what if I can't leave?

What if I'm stuck here . . . forever?

Fear sends its bony fingers down my spine. If I'm caught, I'll be branded a runaway slave. I'll be beaten and whipped. Despite the heat, I begin to shiver. A knot of panic rises up my throat. I swallow it back down and force myself to concentrate on getting out of these woods.

Finally, the trail opens up.

It's now wide enough for Caroline to ride beside me. The puppy limps along, blissfully unaware of any danger. I flick on my iPhone and check the map again.

This looks about right.

Another ten minutes and we'll hit the main road.

Then what?

Make a mad dash for Caroline's plantation and hope to outrun the bounty hunters, or—?

Toward us comes a lantern swinging back and forth. Now and then it stops, as if whoever is holding it is searching for something.

The slave catchers?

I'm about to yell to Caroline to turn around when a sharp whistle pierces the gloom, followed by a voice—a man's voice.

"Lobo, Lobo," he shouts. "Come here, Lobo."

Wolf?

With an excited yelp, the puppy races off so fast that you'd never know it had an injured paw.

"There you are," the man says. "Good puppy."

Setting down his lantern, he scoops the puppy into his arms. As it licks his face, I can see that he's not a man—he's a boy, probably not that much older than I am. Eighteen, maybe. He wears a light shirt and dark trousers tucked into tall boots. The moon highlights his silvery blond hair.

Caroline gives a little cry. "Theo?"

He looks up. Caroline jumps off Allegra and rushes toward him. He fends her off while still holding onto the puppy.

"Sorry, ma'am," he says. "But—"

Caroline seems to fold into herself. "I thought you were my brother."

While the boy apologizes again, I grab Allegra's reins before she has a chance to wander off. In the distance, I hear men's voices—still rowdy with booze—and wheels rumbling over dirt. That cart has caught up to us. Good thing this boy—whoever he is—slowed us down, otherwise we'd be totally cooked.

"Hush," I say.

Even the puppy goes quiet.

The cart trundles past, and though I can't see it, I can imagine it how it looks—a dirty wooden buckboard with a weasel-faced driver whipping his tired horse and a couple of slaves, bound and gagged, in the back.

From Caroline's expression, I think she's imagining it, too. And I'm not sure, but judging by the frown on his face, I'd hazard a guess that so is the boy.

"What's your name?" I ask, as Spinner jiggles his bit. Like me, he's anxious to get out of here.

"Gideon Palmer," the boy replies. "I'm from—"

"Boston?" I say.

He looks at me. "How could you tell?"

I burst out laughing. Nerves, probably, but also because his accent is just like home. When my father's grandparents emigrated from Holland, they settled in Boston. Dad grew up there.

Caroline cuts in. "I'm Caroline Chandler, and this is my friend"—she waves in my direction—"Samantha DeVries."

"Pleased to meet you," Gideon says.

He doesn't seem the least bit fazed by running into a couple of girls on a lonely trail in the middle of the night. Maybe he's a time traveler, too. Okay, that's wishful thinking, but you never know.

He says, "Are you lost?"

"No," Caroline says. "We're going home."

"This is an odd time to be doing it," Gideon Palmer says. "But—"

"—whatever floats your boat?" I say.

He laughs. "That's a good way of putting it."

I'm beginning to like this guy. He's cradling the puppy as if it's his favorite stuffed toy. "He's a keeshond, right?" I say.

"I don't rightly know," Gideon says, looking thoughtful. "Lobo belongs to the major."

26

CAROLINE

Mississippi, July 1863

MAJOR . . . THE UNION ARMY . . . and the soldiers who've taken over my house. This Gideon Palmer must be one of them.

A Yankee.

And to think I almost threw my arms around him, mistaking him for Theo. They're both slender with fair hair and friendly smiles, but it's too dark for me to see the color of Mr. Palmer's eyes.

No, not Mister.

He'll be something else. A corporal or a sergeant.

"Are you a sergeant?" I say.

He gives a little bow. "Nothing so grand, I'm afraid. I'm a lowly second lieutenant."

Knowing nothing about army ranks, I nod and take Allegra's reins from Sam. If only I could leap onto my horse's back the way she does. Maybe if I wasn't wearing this stupid riding habit, I'd—

"Wait up," Sam says.

She hitches her right leg over Spinner's withers and is about to slide off to help me when Gideon Palmer steps forward. He sets down the puppy, still a wriggling mass of happy fur. "May I be of assistance?"

"Yes"—I hesitate—"and thank you."

"My pleasure," the lieutenant says, lifting me up so vigorously that I almost land on the other side of Allegra. She sidesteps, which makes it even more precarious. I clutch at her mane and, for once, I wish I had a saddle.

"That'll teach you," Sam says, laughing. "I bet—"

Someone yells, "There she is, boys. Let's get her."

Flaming torches pierce the night as three riders bear down on us so fast there's no time to think, let alone escape. A vicious kick sends Gideon Palmer into the ditch. Spinner rears, hooves flashing like a wild-eyed war horse. Sam clings to his neck, even more wild-eyed than he is.

"Run for it," I shout, but too late.

A man rides his horse between us; another throws a rope around Sam and trusses her up like a chicken. She kicks and screams, but this time she's no match for him. He snatches at Spinner's reins.

"Got you," Mr. Kelley snarls. "You cain't git away now."

How did he get free?

Someone must've found him not long after we left, and

he'd come chasing after us but bumped into the slave catchers instead. Together, they obviously figured out that we'd taken a short cut, and—

With a vicious squeal, Sam's horse whips around and sinks his teeth into Mr. Kelley's thigh.

"Go, Spinner!" Sam cries.

The overseer smashes her mouth with his fist. "Shut up, you—"

Blood spurts from Sam's lips. The lieutenant lurches to his feet and rushes forward, but he gets knocked down again. These men are twice his size and ten times as mean. I kick Allegra, hard, and try to ram into Mr. Kelley. His filthy boot rams into me instead.

"Stay out of this, Miz Caroline," he says. "You got no business here."

"Mr. Hamilton will punish you for this."

Mr. Kelley spits. "No, he'll punish you for stealing his horse."

Eyes gleaming like a maniac, he jerks his rope even tighter around Sam. Another man gags her with a filthy rag. She throws herself from side to side, then gives me a last desperate look before being dragged away.

Like a slave.

"No, no," I shriek. "You can't—"

But my words are cut off when Mr. Kelley's whip snakes around my arm and yanks me off my horse. I land with a thud next to Gideon Palmer, and the last thing I hear is a Rebel yell as Mr. Kelley and his slave catchers vanish as if the woods have swallowed them whole.

Gideon struggles to sit up.

The moon is so bright that I can see a large bump on his forehead. "They've taken Sam," I say, barely able to get the words out. I want to race after them, but that would be foolish. If I'm going to rescue Sam, I need to stay free. I need to think of a plan—and I need help.

"Slave catchers," Gideon says.

"Worse," I say. "It was the overseer."

Despite the heat, I shiver and try to think logically. Mr. Kelley won't take Sam back to the Hamiltons' plantation because they're about to leave for Biloxi and the last thing they need right now is another slave.

No, Mr. Kelley will take Sam somewhere else.

But where?

It takes a few moments for the obvious answer to leap into my befuddled head.

My house.

Mr. Kelley is tighter than a tick with my father's overseer. They've collaborated before, catching runaway slaves and earning large rewards. But Sam doesn't have an owner to hand out a large reward, so while Mr. Kelley is riding south with the Hamiltons, Zeke Turner will be dragging Sam to the slave auction.

But first, he will beat her.

My fists curl into balls. Angry tears stream down my face. All I can think of is Sam huddled on the dirt floor of a slave cabin, being kicked and whipped. Without Papa to curtail him, Zeke Turner will be brutal. He'll unleash all his vicious fury on my dearest friend.

How did I not see this before?

Shame joins my angry tears. I'm angry with myself, and I'm ashamed of the world I've inhabited all my life without seeing it for what it really is.

Beside me, Gideon says, "I'm sorry."

"What for?"

"For not being a good soldier," he says, looking so much like Theo that it almost breaks my heart. "But I'm really new at this. I should have defended you and your friend. What's her name again?"

"Sam," I say. "Samantha De—"

I've already said too much. Slaves don't have last names, and for my cover story to work, I need to backtrack. But Gideon carries on as if my words didn't register.

"Tell me about her," he says, still cuddling the puppy.

So I do . . . up to a point.

But I hold off about Sam being a time traveler, because without her iPhone to prove it, Gideon Palmer will think I'm a crackpot. So I spin a tale about Sam being a free black girl from the North who ended up down here, and now she's been captured.

Illegally.

Gideon offers to help. "But first," he says, looking at his watch, "I need to sleep and so do you."

"I can't."

"You'll be of no use to your friend unless you do."

Tomorrow, he wants me to come to the house—*my* house—to meet the major, but I'm nervous. I don't trust Union soldiers even if I'm beginning to agree with them and their cause. Struggling to my feet, I catch Allegra—happily snacking on leaves from low hanging branches—and ask Gideon for a leg-up.

Just then, his lantern flickers and goes out.

27

SAMANTHA

Mississippi, July 1863

KEEPING PACE WITH THE OVERSEER, Spinner races through the woods. If he falters or slows down, I'll end up on the ground being dragged like a sack of potatoes. Finally, the trail spills into the main road. Rough hands drag me off Spinner's back and toss me onto the buckboard. I land hard. Splinters pierce my cheeks, my elbows, and my knees.

Fury boils in my brain.

The overseer's whip cracks like a thunderbolt, but I curl myself into a ball and roll away. I hear him coiling the whip, getting ready to strike again, when a voice cuts in.

"Stop!"

"Outta my way, boys," says Mr. Kelley. "This one is mine, and—"

There's a scuffle, the dull sound of punches and grunts. Men fighting. Two against one, I'm guessing.

The slave catchers win.

"Here's your share," one of them says, and I sense that money is changing hands. "Now, go on home, y'hear? We're taking this little filly to Zeke Turner. He pays more'n you do"—there's a lengthy pause—"especially for a filly with no marks on her."

Through half-closed eyes, I see Mr. Kelley whirling his horse around to snatch at Spinner's reins. My fingers are crossed that he'll bite the overseer again. Better yet, I hope Spinner breaks free and gallops off to a new home. With a lurch, the buckboard rumbles forward, rattling and banging over ruts big enough to loosen its wheels.

Every inch of me hurts.

My arms chafe against rough rope, my legs are screaming from hanging onto Spinner, and my face feels like it did when I took a flyer off Nugget over a cross-country fence and landed headfirst in two inches of gravel.

With both arms tied, I'm unable to steady myself, so I roll from one side of the wagon to the other. After what seems like an hour, but is probably less than twenty minutes, the wagon tilts violently and crashes to a halt. I almost fall out.

"Told ya that wheel was busted," says a voice.

"Shaddup," says the other. "Git that horse unhitched."

If it wasn't real, this would be almost funny. Think "Dumb and Dumber" or circus clowns with big red noses and baggy pants who keep tripping over their floppy shoes.

Two pairs of rough hands haul me from the wagon and hoist me onto the cart horse, still in its harness and traces. The stiff leather surcingle digs into my thighs; the horse's bony withers cut into me like a dull knife. If I had reins and if this were Spinner, I could escape. They'd never be able to outrun me. But this poor old horse has barely enough strength to put one foot in front of the other—kind of like the way I feel right now.

I bite down hard on fear.

These men aren't going to whip me. But Zeke Turner will. Caroline told me about him. She said he's meaner than Mr. Kelley. I mull over my escape options—pretty thin on the ground right now—as we plod through the gloom toward Caroline's plantation.

Will she get there before us?

That Gideon Palmer looked like a decent guy. Maybe he'll help get me out of this mess, that is, if Caroline can convince him I need saving.

Dawn is yet to come when we stop. Below a still brilliant moon, I see huts with thatched roofs and scraggly picket fences. There's no sign of life. If anyone heard us coming, they're hiding inside. The same rough hands that hoisted me onto the cart horse drag me off again. Landing badly, I collapse in a heap.

"Git up, you stupid—"

They drag me into a hut, rip off my boots, and dump me on the dirt floor. I smell decay and fear. Something with tiny feet skitters over my legs.

A rat?

The door closes. There's no sound of a lock being clicked, no metal bolt being slid into place. But it doesn't make any difference. I couldn't get out of these ropes even if I had a knife, which I don't.

I am trapped.

My only hope is for Caroline to rescue me before Zeke Turner shows up or for me to figure out how I got here in the first place and then get the heck out. I don't know much about time travel, not like Erik does, but I know enough to realize that I've traveled through some sort of portal. So what was I doing in real time that shunted me back to the Civil War as if I'd stepped into a magic school bus or *Dr. Who*'s TARDIS?

Okay, I was in a bed. Caroline's bed. No, not Caroline's. It belongs to Hughie-Dewey and his transparent wife.

Is *that* the time portal?

I doubt it, otherwise a bazillion other people would've had the same experience. What was it that made mine unique? I remember when my brother had hives and Mom went on a mission to rule out whatever it was that caused them. She tested this against that, came up blank, and tested again. Finally, she figured out that he couldn't tolerate strawberries of all things.

No strawberries here.

Just me, my cell phone, and my earbuds, which I'm surprised nobody's found. They haven't dug into my pockets or frisked me like a criminal. Maybe that's the combination— Hughie-Dewey's spare bed and a cell phone.

But that's crazy.

I bet all his guests have cell phones, and if any other people had mysteriously disappeared, that bedroom would've made headlines. It would be a major tourist attraction with glossy brochures at the airport and a video on Hughie-Dewey's web site. There has to be something else, some oddball detail I'm missing.

So, what was it?

Despite the filthy gag, I yawn. Sleep overcomes me and I drift into dreams filled with gargoyles and dragons that are even worse than what I'm already dealing with.

~ 28 ~

CAROLINE

Mississippi, July 1863

STRIKING A MATCH, Gideon Palmer relights his lantern
and then gives me another leg-up. He is gentler this time, and
I land like a whisper on Allegra's comfortable back.

Mama would be horrified.

I have no saddle and no chaperone, and I'm accompanied
by a young man I've only just met. Even worse, he's a Union
soldier and I'm tempted to invite him to ride behind me. But
he needs to stay on the ground so he can keep the major's
puppy from running off again.

"Tell me about the major," I say. "Is he in charge?"

"Yes."

"Why not a general?" I gather up my reins. Allegra
dances about, eager to get going. "I thought those were the
chief soldiers."

"We're only half a battalion," Gideon says, striding along beside me. "The major's taken charge because we lost our colonel"—he catches his breath—"and a lot of other men at Vicksburg."

"So did we," I say, wishing I'd paid more attention to what Papa had told Louise and me. "Why did you take over our house?"

"Because the men are exhausted. They need a place to rest before—"

"Killing more of our soldiers?"

"We didn't start this war," Gideon says.

I narrow my eyes. "Then who did?"

"Slave owners," he says, spitting out the words. "My father's a lawyer and an abolitionist. He helps slaves get away from places like this." There's a pause. "And he'll help Sam, too. I promise."

"But she's *not* a slave."

"I could tell," he says. "But those criminals who just caught her don't care about that. They see the color of somebody's skin, and that's all they need."

The trail ends abruptly, and now we're back on the main road. With few trees to hide it, the moon shines big and bright like a harvest moon. Sam told me that men have already walked on its surface. I want to believe her, but that's a bit far-fetched, even for me. If only I had Sam's iPhone, I'd be able to tell Gideon Palmer the truth, but I doubt it would make any difference. If he's an abolitionist like his father, he'll want to help rescue Sam no matter what century she comes from.

The puppy flops into a heap, tongue lolling out and looking up hopefully at Gideon. He scoops Lobo into his arms. Even with all that fur, I doubt he weighs much more than a large cat.

"Lobo?" I say. "That's an odd name."

"It's Spanish for 'wolf.'"

"Is the major Spanish?" I say.

Theo told me that the North has recruited foreign soldiers, including Zouaves from Algeria, who wear baggy trousers and embroidered jackets instead of proper uniforms.

"No, I think he's Dutch."

I almost blurt out that Sam is, too—well, her father's family is—but that would only contradict my story and confuse the lieutenant. I glance down and see the top of his head. He's got a cowlick, just like Theo's.

"Did you meet my brother?" I say.

Gideon nods. "He's with your parents and your sister. The major gave them a safe conduct pass."

"Where to?"

"New Orleans."

"Aunt Maude," I whisper. "That's where I will go."

"Alone?" Gideon says.

"No, with Sam."

But only if she's still around. I don't want her to leave, but I will cheer like crazy if she's able to time travel out of this century, away from Zeke Turner's whip and cruel hands.

And away from me.

A sob catches in my throat, and I choke it back because Sam's safety is more important than my feelings. I've never had a best friend before. I'd never even heard the term until

Sam told me about her best friend, Jenna. She showed me pictures on her iPhone, and I gasped over Nugget and Copper—golden chestnuts with flaxen manes and tails, just like Spinner.

"You'd love Jenna," Sam had said. "She reminds me of you."

The road forks. Both trails lead to my house, so which one did the slave catchers take? We need to avoid them.

"This way," Gideon says, taking the right fork. "The other one leads directly to the slave cabins, and I reckon that's where they've taken your friend."

Twenty minutes later we crest the hill. Ahead I see the familiar shape of my house, its barns and outbuildings. In the moon's eerie light, they look different to me now. The slave cabins I once thought were picturesque with their thatched roofs and picket fences are nothing more than thinly disguised jails.

I give a little shudder.

Sam is probably in one of those cabins, being held prisoner. We have to find out which one, but there's nothing we can do until morning when we get Gideon's major involved. I don't want to, because I'm scared, but what choice do I have? Zeke Turner won't listen to me, not without my father here.

"Come to the house," Gideon says. "You'll be more comfortable in a real bed."

I shake my head. "No, I'm going to find my horse, and then I shall sleep in the hayloft."

Gideon Palmer lays a hand on Allegra's warm neck. "You mean this isn't your horse?"

"Allegra belongs to my father," I say, patting her. My hand brushes against Gideon's, and it's not an unpleasant feeling. In fact, it's quite nice. "My mare is called Pandora."

"What color is she?"

"Bay, with a perfect white star."

He groans. "Nobody can get near her."

"Yes!" I punch the air with my fist, startling Allegra and positively shocking Gideon Palmer. This is another of Sam's crazy moves, like high fives and thumbs-ups.

"You're full of surprises," he says.

"Is Pandora in the barn?" I say. If she's still in her stall and won't let anyone get close, then who's feeding her or giving her fresh water?

"She's in the paddock," Gideon says. "Your brother turned her loose before they left." He stoops to let the puppy down. "I've thrown hay over the fence and made sure that her tub is full of water, but—"

"Thank you," I say.

There's a pause. Then he says, "If she won't let anyone get close, why does she belong to you?"

"It's a long story," I say. "And we don't have time for it right now. But in a nutshell, Pandora hates men."

"So we found out," Gideon says. There's another pause, longer this time. "The major's not happy about it. He needs horses his men can ride, but—"

"What?" I pull Allegra to a halt.

The puppy yips, and Gideon scoops him up again. "Nothing."

"Liar," I say, because there's something in his voice that carries a warning. "What's wrong with my horse, apart from the fact that you can't catch her?"

Gideon clears his throat. "We have hundreds of horses to feed, and grain's in short supply," he says. "And our troops are hungry, too. They need meat to keep them in fighting shape."

"No," I gasp. "You don't mean—?"

"This afternoon I overheard the major telling his orderly to give him a list of all the horses that weren't fit for battle."

"Including Pandora?"

"Yes."

Bursting into tears, I grab Allegra's mane and kick her so hard that she rears and I almost slide off her back. But I don't care. I need to get to Pandora, and fast. We take off at a gallop, leaving Gideon and the puppy behind us.

I'm racing past the smokehouse when it happens. Allegra stumbles, and I go flying over her head. From the barn comes a chorus of whinnies, so Allegra trots off to join her old friends and leaves me lying in the dirt. Winded, but not hurt.

Well, except for my pride.

"Are you all right?"

Gideon bends over me. The puppy licks my face. I push him away and wipe my eyes. They're full of grit—and tears. I can't stop crying. Gideon gives me a handkerchief—at least, I think that's what it is—and I blow my nose.

"Thank you. I'll wash it and give it back."

Unfortunately, this makes me cry even harder because I remember Sam saying the same thing to me about wanting to borrow my bloomers.

"No need," Gideon says. "I have plenty more."

He hoists me to my feet and brushes dirt and hay off my skirt. "Thank you," I say again.

"How may I help?" he says.

"Get me a rope from the barn," I say. "I'm going to catch Pandora and put her in a stall—and then I'm going to sleep in it."

"With your horse?"

"I'm not letting her out of my sight until I find Sam and get us out of here."

I've barely finished calling her when Pandora gallops to the paddock gate. She shoves her nose into my hand, whickering softly.

"Sorry, girl," I whisper. "I don't have any treats."

But Pandora doesn't care. She just keeps on nuzzling me with her velvety lips, running them gently up and down my arm the way she always does. Her warm breath is like a promise. Together, we will survive all this. We will find Sam and ride to New Orleans.

Gideon brings me a rope. I wrap it around Pandora's neck and lead her toward the barn, but I hardly need the rope. I could've led her in by her forelock.

"I prepared a stall for you," he says, holding up his lantern.

I cross my fingers—something else Sam taught me—that nobody else is in the barn. Sometimes one of the slaves would sleep in the hayloft, but I doubt they're doing that now—unless there's a Union soldier on guard.

"Did anybody see you?"

"No," Gideon says.

He has filled a water bucket and put fresh hay in the manger. The bedding is thick and clean. Pandora tucks her nose into the hay while I settle myself on a mound of straw. Luckily, this stall is the largest, so there's plenty of room for me and my horse.

"Thank you," I say. "You're very kind."

"Is there anything else can I do?"

I think for a minute. Who can I trust to help us? "Are the slaves still here?"

"Most of them," Gideon says. "A few ran off, but we're paying wages to the ones who stayed behind. One or two can actually write, so—"

Write?

"Find a girl called Pearl," I say. "Send her to me." My stomach rumbles.

"With food?" he says, grinning.

I'm too hungry to feel embarrassed. "Yes, and tell her to bring me breeches and a shirt. She'll know where to find them."

"Will she keep her mouth shut?"

"Oh, yes," I say. "But will you?"

"Of course," he says, with a smile in his voice. "I'll find Pearl, and I'll come back tomorrow at first light."

"It's already tomorrow," I remind him.

He pulls a watch from his pocket. "Oh, yes." There's a pause. "I'll return in a few hours. I hope you sleep well."

And then he's gone.

"Miz Caroline?"

I awake with a start. "Who's there?"

"Pearl, ma'am."

She opens Pandora's door and slips inside. I can just make her out. My horse is lying down, but she barely stirs. Pearl kneels beside me. We are two girls, eye to eye. She hands me a slice of watermelon, and I devour it like I've never eaten before. Juice dribbles down my chin and onto my blouse.

"I have your clothes," Pearl says.

Her diction is so precise it's almost like Sam's but without the modern touch. I remember that diary Pearl was writing in and her quizzical look when I stole those apples. Things between us have shifted.

"Thank you," I say.

Gravely, she nods. "You're most welcome."

Another odd expression for a slave. Where did she learn that? As if she can read my mind, Pearl says, "I've read Jane Austen, ma'am." There's a pause. "And Mr. Longfellow."

"*Evangeline?*" I say.

"No," Pearl replies. "*A Slave's Dream.*"

For a moment, I'm too choked up to speak. So I busy myself with taking the clothes she's brought and eating another slice of watermelon. There's also a slab of cornbread, so

I gobble that down, too. Her hand touches mine and neither of us pulls away. Then Pandora lurches to her feet and Pearl is up first, comforting my mare. She whispers into Pandora's ear. I can't hear her words, but my horse does. She sighs and relaxes.

"Do you remember Sam?" I say.

"The girl in your room?"

"Yes," I say. "Can you find out where she is?"

"Why?"

"Because Zeke Turner has just captured her. She's in one of the slave cabins, and I'm going to rescue her."

I'm no longer touching Pearl, but I can almost feel her shudder. Has she also run amok of Zeke Turner's whip? When I see Papa again, I shall force him to dismiss the overseer. Better yet, I'll insist that Mr. Turner be flogged and thrown into jail.

But no judge in the South would agree.

They're all in cahoots with the slave owners, including my father and Mr. Hamilton. Theo was absolutely right. This war is all wrong.

We are wrong.

"Find Sam," I say. "Tell her"—my voice chokes up again—"tell her I'm getting help."

Silently, Pearl disappears so completely I'm beginning to wonder if I conjured her up. But no. The proof is all around me—Theo's breeches, his white linen shirt, and the sweet taste of watermelon that lingers in my mouth.

❧ 29 ❧

SAMANTHA

Mississippi, July 1863

THORNS RIP MY CLOTHES TO SHREDS as I race
through the woods. Gargoyles with bloody fingers claw my
face. I dodge left, then right, but I can't outrun the dragon
whose fiery breath is now scorching my back. It's about to
grab me, when—

There's a tap on the door.

What door?

There aren't any doors in the woods. Heart thumping like
sneakers in a dryer, I force my eyes to open. The gargoyles
vanish.

"Sam?" calls a voice.

Caroline?

No, it's not her. But it's a voice I've heard before. Slowly,
the door opens and a faint light trickles inside. A girl in a

white turban floats toward me. She drops to her knees and that's when I recognize her.

In a flash, she has my gag off.

I choke and spit. I can barely speak. My mouth is so sore that it feels as if I've gone six rounds in a boxing match.

"Don't talk," Pearl says. "Just listen."

She gives me a sip of water from a jug, then tells me that Caroline's in the barn with Pandora. The lieutenant is firmly on our side, and he'll be getting his major to overrule whatever horror Zeke Turner plans to unleash.

"Untie me," I croak out.

"No." Pearl puts a hand to my swollen lips. "That would get you a beating, for sure," she says. "I figure you're not strong enough to run away, so best you lie here, like before, and trust Miz Caroline to do what needs to be done."

"I'm not a slave," I say.

"Neither am I," Pearl replies, so softly I barely hear her. "I'm a free girl from Illinois."

I don't know much about states' rights, but I'm learning fast. According to the book Caroline sneaked from Mr. Hamilton's library, Illinois outlawed slavery more than thirty years ago, so—

"What happened?" I say.

Pearl catches her breath. "Zeke Turner."

With gentle fingers she ties my gag back on, but loose enough so it doesn't hurt. If she were a modern girl she'd give me a high five or a fist bump and tell me to *Hang in, there.* Instead, Pearl slips through the door so quietly that it's almost as if she wasn't even here at all.

Maybe I only dreamed about her.

❧ 30 ❧

CAROLINE

Mississippi, July 1863

GIDEON WAKES ME AT DAWN. As I pull myself together, horses whinny and stamp their feet, anxious for food. Raven snorts. I stroke his magnificent head.

"I'll get you out of here, I promise."

In the stall beside him, Meteor whickers.

"You, too," I say, stroking his nose as well.

Meteor is my brother's favorite, and I won't leave him behind, either—although how I'm going to get three horses, including a stallion, down to my aunt's house in New Orleans, I haven't yet begun to figure out.

While Gideon fills water buckets from the pump, I measure the horses' grain. I've just about finished when my favorite groom shuffles into the barn. Oscar has been part of my life since before I can remember. I ask him to keep a close eye on Pandora.

"Don't let anyone near her, okay?"

"O-K?" Oscar says, scratching his grizzled head. "Is dat sumpin' I don't know about?"

"It means *all right.*"

"Then, *okay*, Miz Caroline," he says.

In front of the harness room's tiny mirror, I brush hay off my dusty riding habit and do the best I can with my tangled hair. I look a fright, but I really don't give a hoot. I am no longer scared about meeting Gideon's major; I am absolutely furious with him.

"What about Sam?" I ask. "Is she safe?"

"Pearl found her," Gideon says. "And don't worry. I've sent my sergeant to keep Zeke Turner busy while we talk to the major."

"What have you told him?"

"Just that you found Lobo last night and that you need to speak with him."

"With Lobo?" I say.

"No," Gideon says. "With the major."

At another time, this might even be funny. "Does the major know about Sam?"

"No. I thought it best for you to tell him."

He's wearing his uniform—a dark blue jacket with gold buttons and a dark blue cap. It makes him look older, more mature than the boy I met last night. Politely, he offers his arm, and I take it because my legs are none too steady as we walk toward the house.

My house.

The steps could use a good scrub, the windows are filthy, and there are muddy footprints all over Mama's porch. Her tubs of lilies are gasping for water.

Two solders are standing guard, or they would be if they weren't slouched on a wooden bench. One of them manages to stand and salute Gideon. I suppose the other one should, too, but he appears to be snoring. These boys look even more exhausted than Sam Wade did.

"At ease, private," Gideon says.

With a formal bow, he opens the door and ushers me through it. Inside the foyer are more soldiers. One sits at a desk. I look closer. It's not a desk; it's Mama's precious bombé chest. Good thing she's not here to see it covered with dog-eared ledgers and a bowl of half-eaten food.

The soldier nods at Gideon. "The major's in his office."

Office?

Has he moved into Papa's library?

But to my surprise, he's chosen Mama's front parlor. They've pushed her furniture to one side, rolled up the rugs, and piled her porcelain tea cups into a crate that sits beside the fireplace. Above it, Grandmother Abigail's disapproving face is covered with a map of Louisiana and Mississippi. A tiny blue flag sticks up just about where her nose would be.

Mama's heavy drapes are pulled back. This is probably the first time sunlight has ever reached inside this dismal room. A tall man wearing the same uniform as Gideon stands by the open window.

So this is the major who wants to shoot my horse.

Turning sharply, he strides toward me. His spurs rattle; a scabbard clanks against his leg, and there's a handgun tucked into his belt. With all that hardware, it looks as if the major's ready for a fight, and he's going to get one—from me.

"Miss Chandler," he says, holding out his hand. I ignore it. "It's a pleasure to meet you. I'm Nicolas Van Houten."

No mention of rank.

His eyes are a riveting shade of blue, and they bore right through me. He's blond and clean shaven, with a strong chin and high cheekbones; and despite the gold braid on his shoulders, he doesn't look much older than Gideon. In other words, he's not quite the monster I expected. At his feet, the puppy lets out a couple of yips.

"Thank you for finding Lobo," the major says, bending to stroke the puppy's ears, "and for removing the thorn from his paw."

"It wasn't me," I say. "It was my friend, Sam, and you've got to help her."

"Sam?" he says. "Wouldn't that be a boy?"

"Sam's a girl," I say. "And while we're arguing about names, she's probably getting whipped."

Major Van Houten waves me into a ladderback chair, but I remain standing. This is not a social call; we are not about to have tea and discuss the price of cotton.

"As you wish." The major unstraps his sword, then takes a seat behind his desk—my mother's marble-topped table—and looks up at Gideon, standing to attention like a toy soldier. "What's all this about, Lieutenant?"

But before Gideon has a chance to speak, another man rushes into the room with a handful of papers. He drops them on the major's desk and stands back to wait. With what appears to be deliberate slowness, the major puts on his spectacles and begins reading.

"Excuse me," he says.

I slam both fists on Mama's table. "No, I won't."

My father's glass ink well bounces twice, then topples over, spilling Papa's expensive black ink onto the major's papers. He looks up, aggravation written all over his face. Gideon puts a hand on my shoulder. I shake him off.

"I think you owe me an apology," says the major.

I lean toward him. "Wrong, major," I say. "It's *you* who owe me one."

He has the grace to look surprised. "Why?"

"Because you've stolen my house, you're planning to shoot my horse, and my best friend is about to get whipped because she rescued your puppy."

A slight exaggeration, but it gets his attention.

"Lieutenant Palmer," the major says. "Look into this, please."

"I already did, sir."

"And?"

"Miss Chandler's correct. Her friend, Samantha, is being held prisoner by Zeke Turner."

"The overseer?"

"Yes, sir."

The major lets out his breath. "You mean to tell me that this man, this Zeke Turner, is holding a white girl captive?"

"Sam's not white," I burst out. "She's black."

❧ 31 ❧

SAMANTHA

Mississippi, July 1863

SOMETHING WAKES ME. Not a tap on the door this time, but men's voices beyond it. Gruff, angry voices.

Arguing voices.

I recognize the slave catchers—Dumb and Dumber—but the other voice is new. It's rough and demanding, with a nasal twang.

Zeke Turner?

The door bursts open. Light spills onto the floor and almost blinds me. Footsteps approach; I sense someone large and full of menace standing over me. Blinking rapidly, I force myself to focus.

Backlit by the sun, Zeke Turner is every film maker's worst caricature of a Southern overseer—bewhiskered, bug-eyed, and filthy. He chews for a moment, then spits out a stream of tobacco juice that lands in the dirt beside me. Another inch, and it would've hit my face. I shudder.

"Scared, aint'cha," he sneers.

Slowly, he walks around me, poking me with the toe of his boot. Hard, but not hard enough to really hurt. Or maybe I'm just numb all over and can't feel a thing.

"Git her up, boys," he says.

My legs turn to jelly as the slave catchers haul me upright. Zeke Turner rips the gag off my mouth. I'd spit in his eye, but I don't have enough saliva. He grips my sore face, yanks it from side to side, and I try not to wince.

"Well, what have we here?" he drawls. "A slave with blue eyes? I ain't never seen one of them before."

The other two lean closer. Their foul breath turns my stomach. "She's a freak."

"Nah, she's a witch."

"She'll fetch more money." Zeke Turner twists my face again. "But she's a little scratched up."

"Kelley did it," says the one I call Dumb.

Dumber joins in. "Yeah, he wuz gonna whip her, but—"

Still holding me up, Dumb says, "That sergeant, he's comin' over this way. You want me to get rid of him?"

Zeke Turner growls. "I'll take care of it. You stay with her."

The door bangs shut behind him, and I relax. A sergeant means rescue, doesn't it? If I had the strength to cheer, I would. But I'm having trouble standing, even with Dumb and Dumber holding me up. There's a muffled conversation I can't hear, then Zeke Turner crashes back through the door.

"That major wants to see her."

"Now?"

"Yeah," says the overseer.

Dumb looks at him. "Where?"

"At the big house."

They drag me out of the cabin. Fresh air has never smelled so good before. A horse whinnies; birds sing. I hear children playing. Life sounds almost normal except for Dumber, grunting as he pats me down again. I hold my breath, waiting for him to find my iPhone, but his gnarly fingers skate right over it.

"The sergeant says we gotta take her up the back stairs," Zeke Turner goes on, still chewing on his wad of tobacco. "They're sending a slave to clean her up before she meets the major"—he spits—"though he's a damn fool for wantin' to see her."

By a stroke of luck, they drag me into Caroline's room, and I'm tossed onto a bed I know quite well. My arms are still tied, but my mouth is free.

"Where's—?"

"Shaddup," Dumb says, slapping my face.

The door opens, and Pearl floats toward me. I've not been brought up to believe in much of anything except my own sense of values, but right now I'm willing to believe in guardian angels. If Pearl suddenly sprouted wings, I'd offer to fluff them up for her. I'd even polish her halo.

"You know what to do," Zeke Turner says.

Pearl nods. "Yessir."

"Make her look good, y'hear?"

She nods again.

Before leaving, the overseer yanks off my ropes. "Don't try any funny stuff," he warns. "We got a guard on the door and another outside, lessen' you fool enough to climb out the window."

"Fat chance of that," I say, rubbing my arms.

Right now, I don't have the strength to walk, never mind shimmy down a drainpipe. Pearl tells me to lie still, then gently rubs my face with a lotion that smells kind of pungent, like something my mother would buy at the health food store.

I wrinkle my nose. "What is it?"

"Calendula," Pearl replies. "Good for wounds."

She fills a bowl with water from a pitcher, produces a soft cloth out of nowhere, and helps me clean up. I can't believe the dirt that comes off my legs and arms. My feet are beyond filthy.

"Thank you," I say, feeling better already. "How's Caroline? Is she all right?"

"She's fine, but she's worried about you"—there's a pause—"and her horse."

"Pandora?"

Pearl nods. "Seems like the major wants to get rid of the horses his men can't ride. None of them can get near Miz Caroline's mare."

"Go, Pandora," I say.

With a gulp, I think about Spinner. He'd make a great battle horse. Then I remember what Dad said about a million horses being killed in this horrible war. It takes six horses to pull a cannon, two more to pull a supply wagon. Horses carry soldiers into battle, and they make a perfect target. The other side will always shoot an enemy's horse first.

It's easier to hit than a man.

"Now, take off those dirty clothes," Pearl says. "And I'll find something clean. You can't meet the major looking like this."

While she's hunting through Caroline's armoire, I struggle out of my grubby shirt and pull off Theo's torn breeches. Tangled in its earbuds, my iPhone tumbles from Leo's pocket, so I plug myself in.

"Oh," Pearl says, putting a hand to her mouth.

"What?"

Wide-eyed, she points at my *Barn Bratz* tank top. It's ridden up again, and I'm not wearing bloomers because I'd ditched them before we left the Hamilton's plantation. Bloomers and breeches don't play nice with each other, not if you want to ride a horse and be comfortable. I yank my tank top down. "Sorry."

Just like it happened with Caroline.

And that's when the penny drops.

Or the dime does. How could I have been so dumb? Clutching my iPhone, I lurch off the bed and hobble to the dresser. Where's that glass jar? Did somebody steal it? There was a good chunk of change in there. Frantically, I poke about and find it buried beneath a muddle of petticoats and bonnets that Caroline left behind.

Now where's my dime?

Without thinking, I upend the jar. Nickels, pennies, and

dimes bounce across Caroline's bed. Too late, I realize that my dime would've been on top.

"What are you looking for?" Pearl says.

"A dime."

"Plenty of those here," she says. Her slender fingers dance among the coins. She looks at one, discards it, then looks at ten more. A whole dollar's worth. "Is this it?"

It shines brighter than the others. I screw up my eyes and peer at the date—1863. Good enough for me. If it doesn't work, I'll try another. With trembling fingers, I take the dime. I turn it around and around, and then I stretch out on the bed with my iPhone and my earbuds.

Is anything missing?

Yes, Lady Gaga, so I tune her in. This is exactly how I got here, but will it take me home again?

"If I disappear, Caroline will explain," I tell a puzzled Pearl. "Tell her that I said good-bye, and"—a tear rolls down my cheek—"tell her that I'll remember her forever, okay?"

Slowly, Pearl nods. "Okay."

Guilt washes over me. I shouldn't be leaving Caroline in the lurch, but she has Gideon now, and I might never have another chance to get home. I have to take it.

So I close my eyes . . . and hope.

32

CAROLINE

Mississippi, July 1863

WITH INFURIATING CALM, Major Van Houten shakes my father's ink off his papers, dismisses the soldier who brought them in, and begins reading again, as if my outburst is of no importance.

"Aren't you going to do *anything*?" I shout.

He gives a little shrug. "We prefer not to get involved with—"

And that's when I lose it. Whatever common sense I have left flies right out the window. I know this won't help my case, but I don't care any more. I will force this idiot major to listen even if I have to beat him into it. Again, I slam my fists on the table.

Gideon steps forward. "Caroline, this isn't—"

"What?" I say, rounding on him.

He steps back. "It's not the right way to go about it."

"You mean there are *rules* for this?"

"Well, yes."

"*Pappekak!*" I yell.

It's a Dutch word that Sam taught me, and it looks as if the major understands because his mouth is now half open. Good. This means I've finally gotten his attention. I press my advantage.

"You're a soldier," I say, snatching his scabbard off the floor. "You have this and a gun, so use them on Zeke Turner. He's vermin."

"He's a man."

"Hardly," I say. "Now are you going to do something about this, or do I—?"

"Put down that sword," the major says. "You'll hurt yourself."

"No, major," I say. "I'm going to hurt *you*."

The sword is heaver than I expected, but somehow I manage to pull it from the scabbard and wave it past his beaky nose. The major doesn't move a muscle.

He just stares at me.

So I drive the point home by stabbing Mama's velvet chaise. A wad of stuffing bursts out. Not quite the effect I was going for, but close enough. If I could reach the major's gun, I'd grab that, too.

"Lieutenant Palmer," he says, sounding a lot calmer than he ought to. "Take care of this matter. Immediately."

Gideon takes a step toward me.

"No, not Miss Chandler," says the major. "Send someone down to bring"—he hesitates—"her servant up to the house."

"Sam's not a servant," I yell. "She's my—"

The major waves me off. "I have work to do here, so have them put her in a room upstairs," he says to Gideon. "And tell them to use the back entrance. I don't want—" His voice trails off.

Gideon salutes. "Yes, sir."

"Wait," I say. "I'm going with you."

"Not so fast, young lady," says the major. "You will stay right here."

"You can't order me about," I yell. "You are *not* my father."

The major sighs. "Thank goodness."

There's an awkward silence, then Gideon salutes again and heads for the door. His hand brushes against mine, and in that brief touch, I sense a message—probably a warning to keep my mouth shut.

But I can't.

"As soon as Sam is free," I tell the major, "we're taking three—no, make that four—of my horses to New Orleans, and you're going to give us safe passage like you did for my parents. Better yet," I say, "you will send soldiers to guard us. Six will do fine, thank you." And then I sit down because my legs have finally given out.

"Are you quite finished?" he says.

"Not yet."

"What else?"

"Zeke Turner," I say. "You will flog him, and then you will lock him up and throw away the key."

"He will be dealt with," the major says, removing his spectacles and placing them on the table. "Now I want you to answer a question."

"Very well."

"Why should I listen to you?"

His mouth twitches; there's a hint of humor in his eyes. He's gotten over his anger, and now he's regarding me the way all men do—as if I'm nothing more than a foolish young woman who cares only for gossip and the latest fashions.

Maybe it's time to play my trump card, but it'll only work if Zeke Turner hasn't found Sam's iPhone and stomped on it. I cross my fingers and hope.

"I'm waiting," says the major.

I suck in my breath. "You should listen to me because I know something about this war that you don't."

Of course, he laughs.

33

SAMANTHA

Mississippi, present day

HARDLY DARING TO BREATHE, I look around Caroline's room. The window fan hums, my suitcase is exactly where I left it, and the digital alarm says three o'clock.

The same time I fell asleep.

Does this mean that time hasn't moved? Did it remain perfectly still while I was gone? Feeling dizzy, I climb off Caroline's bed and stagger to the window. Outside, I see my father strolling toward the barn with Hughie-Dewey; our rental car is still parked in the driveway, ugly as ever.

I put a hand to my face.

No scratches. My arms don't have any rope burns, either, and there are no bruises on my legs from Zeke Turner's vicious boots. Life is back to normal—well, except for the magic dime I'm still clutching.

Can life really turn on a dime?

My hand begins to tingle, so I drop the dime into my knapsack's side pocket. It'll be safe there—for now. Nugget's pedigree, now a bit crumpled, is still in the main compartment. Smoothing it out on the bed, I run my finger down the list of his ancestors.

A familiar name catches my eye.

It's on the last row, and barely legible because I did a rotten job of photocopying the original.

Pandora?

I look again, then count the rows and try to figure out the generations. Math's not my strongest subject, so I do it over. I count from the bottom up, then from the top down again—and wind up in exactly the same place.

The middle 1800s.

This can't be real. It's a crazy, mixed-up dream. I've had them before, so believable and so scary, they've left me shaking in my shoes. But this one was different and now I'm desperate to know if what happened did actually happen.

Did I bring anything back with me?

I hunt around for a clue—something tangible that would prove where I've been—but it's just me, my iPhone, and that dime I won't be touching again. At least, not when I've got my earbuds in.

Something smells.

It can't be me because I just had a shower, like ten minutes ago. Maybe this tank top isn't as clean as I thought it was. I look down. There's a stain I never noticed before, right over the *B* in *Bratz*.

A *wet* stain.

Water? From my shower?

No, it's oily and it smells like that lotion Pearl put on my face—in my dream, of course. What was it called? *Cal*-something-or-other. Calendar? I grab my iPhone, and Wikipedia tells me that *calendula*—yes, that was it—comes from a marigold plant and is an old remedy for healing wounds.

So how did it get on my tank top?

And that's when I notice that my iPhone's battery is more than half gone. It was fully charged when I went to sleep or whatever it was that I did. Holding my breath, I look at Nugget's pedigree again.

Pandora.

And the name beside hers, *Hyperion.*

Their offspring—a mare—is listed as Black Pearl, and I remember Caroline telling me that Pandora had never been bred, so this means that Black Pearl was foaled after I left.

Black Pearl?

It finally sinks in. This wasn't a dream, it was real. I time traveled to 1863 and if I don't go back and help Caroline get Pandora to safety, Nugget might not even exist.

My fingers itch to text Jenna about this, but how do you casually explain you've just spent a week in the Civil War teaching a Southern belle about iTunes and being chased by slave catchers?

Okay, I'll call Erik.

But he doesn't answer, and this isn't something you leave on voice mail. How about Mom? If I tell her what's been going on, she'll freak out and insist I come home right away. As for Dad, he'll laugh and tell me to stop kidding around.

But I'm not kidding.

I'm dead serious. It really happened, and I need to get back to 1863. This time, I need to be armed, not with a gun or a knife, but with information for Gideon's major, whoever he is.

Somehow, I've got to convince the major to help Caroline. Pearl said he was planning to get rid of horses his soldiers couldn't use, and that would include Pandora.

No, no. That must not happen.

Yes, I know this is all speculation and that obviously Pandora survived, because if she hadn't, Nugget wouldn't be here. But what was it that saved her?

Was it me, traveling back to help?

Erik would say yes.

Okay, my brother's a space cadet, and right now I wish he were here. But he isn't, so I have to figure it out for myself. What would he tell me?

Think, Sam, think.

One of Erik's time travel books involved a history professor who dodged execution by convincing a medieval king that he could predict the future. Well, of course, he could, because he was back in the past and he knew exactly what would happen in the future. So, how much do I know about the Civil War?

The North won; Lincoln was shot.

But that didn't happen until 1865. I need something that's about to happen, like right then, in Caroline's time. Plugging my iPhone into its charger, I log on to Google. There are a bazillion sites about the Civil War—firearms and

uniforms and re-enactments galore. I click on a time line—
July, 1863.

First, it was Gettysburg, then the surrender at Vicksburg,
which I know about because Caroline told me. Okay, so what
came next? I go back and forth, checking dates, and discover
that there was a battle in South Carolina at a place called Fort
Wagner in the middle of July.

So I dig further and up comes a movie.

Glory.

It's about a regiment of black soldiers from Boston, and
nobody thinks they're capable of fighting until they storm
Fort Wagner. The web site says:

> *Although a tactical defeat, the publicity of the battle of*
> *Fort Wagner led to further action for black troops in the*
> *Civil War, and it spurred additional recruitment that*
> *gave the Union Army a further numerical advantage in*
> *troops over the South.*

Another detail catches my eye. The actor who plays the
white colonel in charge of the black troops is Matthew Brod-
erick, and he looks almost exactly like the real colonel.

Robert Gould Shaw.

I tuck his name into memory, and then I devour details
about the film, about the soldiers and the battle. But that's not
enough. I need to show Gideon's major what actually happened, and I can't do that with live streaming. I need to down-
load this film.

All it takes is a single click.

With luck, the charge won't show up on Mom's credit

card until after I get home and can explain why I needed a movie about the Civil War.

Home?

Will I be able to get back?

Of course, I will. I did it just now, and I can do it again. But first I have to pack a few essentials, then I need to learn the layout of this house, especially the back stairs that Caroline said the servants used. So far I only know her bedroom, the upstairs hall, and the foyer, and those won't help if I need to get outside unseen.

Okay, what to take?

Underpants and a sports bra. There are two in my suitcase, and one still has tags on it. Perfect. I'll give it to Caroline, and she can start a new fashion. I stuff them into my knapsack, along with a toothbrush and toothpaste and my favorite shampoo. I'll leave that with Caroline, too. The soap she uses to wash her hair is awful.

It's way too hot for jeans, so I climb into cargo shorts, swap my tank top for a plain t-shirt, and open the door. Cautiously, I look up and down the hall.

Nobody around.

Dad's outside with Hewie-Dewey, and I'm guessing that Carrie's still at play practice. But what about Transparent Woman? Maybe she's taking a nap. Tiptoeing past the ancestors, I wink at Caroline's portrait.

"See you soon," I whisper.

The second floor is larger than I expected. After three wrong turns, I finally find a door to the back stairs. They're steep, dark, and narrow, and I cross my fingers that they're still in the same place as they were a hundred and fifty years ago. I check my watch—almost four-thirty.

Time for me to get going.

My brother says there are no rules for time travel, and I hope he's right. Because if there are any rules, I think I'm about to break them—or at least seriously bend them out of shape.

It's now Friday.

Tomorrow, in Caroline's world, the soldiers will attack Fort Wagner. Will I get back in time to dazzle the major with my predictions, or will I be too late?

34

CAROLINE

Mississippi, July 1863

BURSTING INTO MAMA'S PARLOR, Gideon gives the
major a hasty salute. "She's disappeared."

"Who?" the major says, looking up.

He's already pegged me as a hysterical female and has
gone back to working on his papers. He's been reading and
signing them, laboriously, with my father's ink and his quill
pen. Doesn't the Union Army have pens of its own?

"Samantha," Gideon says. "Miss Chandler's friend."

"You mean she's run off?"

Gideon hesitates. "No, she just, sort of, vanished."

"How?" I say, feigning surprise.

But inside, I'm smiling because I know the answer. Sam's
found a way back to her own time. I just wish we'd had a

chance to say good-bye. She's safe now, away from Zeke Turner and his slave catchers.

And away from me.

Catching my breath, I check my pocket for Gideon's handkerchief. I may need it at any moment.

Gideon shakes his head. "I don't know."

"Lieutenant," the major says, "that's not good enough. People don't just disappear."

"This one did." I snap my fingers. "Poof."

They look at me as if I'm utterly insane. Major Van Houten accuses me of making it all up, about Sam being captured and held prisoner by Zeke Turner. Then the major turns on Gideon and lambastes him as well. Now we're both in trouble.

"You've wasted my time," the major says.

With an elaborate sigh, he gets to his feet and has just started on a lecture about responsibility, which sounds frighteningly like the ones Mama delivered on a regular basis, when an orderly races into the room.

He hands the major a telegram.

At least, that's what I think it is. I've seen them before—slips of pale yellow paper from the American Telegraph Company covered with handwriting or typescript. My father got one two months ago from a horse breeder in Virginia.

But this one looks official.

The major drops it onto Mama's marble-topped table. Gideon steps closer. "Bad news, sir?"

"No, it's good," the major says. "We're about to attack Fort Wagner in South Carolina."

"When?"

"Tomorrow night."

"What regiment, sir?"

"Fifty-fourth Massachusetts."

Gideon lets out a low whistle. "That's an all-black regiment, sir."

"Yes," the major says. "I know the colonel in charge. He's a good man. I'm sure he'll take Fort Wagner without any trouble."

I have no idea where Fort Wagner is, but I know that South Carolina's on our side. Or it was, until I switched.

When did that happen?

Gideon says, "Permission to escort Miss Chandler back to the barn, sir?"

"Denied," says the major. "As of this minute, Miss Chandler is confined to the house. She may avail herself of any rooms my men aren't using." There's a pause. "And your job, Lieutenant, is to make sure she obeys."

I'm about to object, when Gideon takes my arm and squeezes it hard. Another message. So I nod politely at the major, but inside I am boiling mad. I am also hungry, and right now I'd kill for a plate of sausages and grits.

But first I need to find Pearl.

She's the only one who knows what happened to Sam—unless Zeke Turner's guards were there as well.

"Follow me," I tell Gideon the moment we're clear of the major.

"Where?"

"Upstairs."

Gideon looks a little shocked, and I know that Mama would be reaching for her smelling salts at the thought of me even talking to a young man, never mind bringing him up to my room. But I've already broken so many rules in the past week, I no longer care.

As if she's been expecting us, Pearl opens my bedroom door. Slipping inside, I give her a quick hug, and she doesn't seem surprised at that, either.

"Tell me what happened," I say. "From the beginning."

So she does, and I clench my fists as she describes the ropes, the cuts on Sam's face, and Zeke Turner's guards.

"Where are they now?" I ask.

"Gone."

"Did they see Sam disappear?"

"No," she says.

"Phew." The last thing we need is Zeke Turner and his slave catchers accusing Pearl—or me—of witchcraft. "So tell me how Sam did it."

"I don't rightly know," Pearl says. "She found a dime in that jar you keep. Then she lay down on the bed with that thing attached to her ears."

"What thing?" Gideon says.

He's leaning against the door. On the other side, I hear soldiers tramping up and down the hall, shouting orders to one another. Seems as if they've taken over every room upstairs except this one.

"Sam's iPhone," I tell him.

"What's that?"

"I'll explain in a minute," I say. "Now, go on, Pearl."

"She said to tell you good-bye and that she'll remember you forever."

"Oh," I say, sniffing. I pull out Gideon's handkerchief, but not fast enough. Tears stream down my face like a water-fall. I can't stop them coming—and right now, I don't want to.

Pearl says, "Then Sam disappeared. One minute she was there; the next she wasn't."

There's an awed silence as we all try to wrap our brains around this. I'm the only one who has any idea what happened to Sam, and even I'm having trouble believing what Pearl just told us.

Between sobs, I tell Pearl and Gideon about Sam's life in the future—her family, the amazing inventions, and how she didn't believe in time travel until it happened to her.

Gideon frowns. "I've read about this."

"You have?"

"It's fantasy, of course," he says. "A fairy tale."

"Not," I say, waving toward my empty bed. "Sam was here, and now she's gone. Pearl watched her disappear, and that's all the proof we need that time travel isn't a fantasy. It's real. You just need the right whatever-it-is to make it happen."

"The dime?" Pearl says.

She catches on fast. I've been puzzling over this myself. It can't be the bed or Sam's iPhone or even her crazy tank top. So it has to be the dime—or a combination of all three.

"Yes," I say. "That's probably it."

Gideon looks about ready to argue when there's a shout

from outside. I race to the window. Oscar is leading Pandora toward the paddock, and two soldiers are trying to stop him. One carries a whip.

"No," I yell.

But they can't hear me because the window is closed. I try to pull it up, but the latch is stuck. Whirling around, I race for the door.

"What's wrong?" Gideon says, grabbing me.

I shake him off. "They're taking Pandora."

"You can't go outside."

"Try to stop me."

With an almighty shove, I push Gideon out of my way and yank open the door. Soldiers stand back, open-mouthed, as I fly down the stairs faster than I ever did before. I hear someone behind me, Gideon probably, but I don't turn to look.

I race past the soldier at Mama's table, through the open front door, and leap off the porch steps like a gazelle. I hit the ground running. There's now quite a crowd around my horse. She rears and strikes out. Men scatter like chickens.

Nostrils flaring, Pandora pins her ears and lunges forward with Oscar still hanging onto her lead rope. She's covered in sweat, her eyes are showing white.

"Outta my way, miss," a soldier says.

I grab his whip. "Oscar, let her go."

He drops the rope, and Pandora takes off. It's dangerous, galloping with a loose rope, but getting shot is far worse. My mare disappears behind the barn—safe, for now—so I turn on the soldier who's aiming his rifle. "Put that down."

"But she's a killer," he says.

"Yeah," says another. "She bit my arm yesterday."

"Don't worry, miss," says a voice from the crowd. "Private O'Malley couldn't hit the side of a barn, never mind a horse."

Laughter breaks out. Then Gideon marches up, looking every inch the commanding officer, which I suppose he is, given that there's no sign of the major or anyone else with gold braid on their shoulders.

"At ease, men," Gideon says.

While he's busy with the soldiers, I slip away to catch Pandora. But somehow Pearl has gotten there first. She's feeding an apple to my horse, stroking her nose and whispering words I can't hear. Pandora nuzzles her hand, as sweet and friendly as the major's puppy.

Pearl hands me the rope. "Are you in trouble?"

"Probably," I say. "And thank you for—"

Pandora's head jerks up. She gives a nervous whinny and dances sideways, almost treading on my feet. I whip around—and there, striding toward us, is Major Van Houten.

35

SAMANTHA

Mississippi . . .

I'M ALMOST READY TO LEAVE. My green knapsack is packed, I'm plugged into my iPhone, and I'm reaching for the magic dime when I hesitate.

Wait a minute.

I can't wear a t-shirt and Old Navy shorts if I want to sneak around the Chandlers' house without being noticed. For that, I'll need something that Pearl would wear—a turban or a straw hat; a burlap skirt.

Ripping out my earbuds, I jump off Caroline's bed and head for the closet. On the door is a full-length mirror. Inside the closet are garment bags that jostle for space with wooden hangers. My hand falls on a gray muslin dress.

This might work.

No, it's got too much lace—not suitable for a slave. Neither is that tie-dye top. But what about this gauzy brown skirt? Nobody will notice the embroidered pattern at the hem or the ties with brass bobbles. I'll just tuck them inside.

From the closet's top shelf, I pull down a cotton scarf that I practice wrapping around my head. The mirror tells me it's not very neat, but it'll do the trick. So will this white peasant blouse. I stuff them all into my bag. Just to be safe, I strip off my cargo shorts and put my tank top back on.

Okay. I think I'm finally ready.

Clutching the dime, I tune in Lady Gaga and wait.

I don't know how long it takes. A few minutes, an hour? I look around Caroline's familiar bedroom, trying to figure out if it's even the same day as when I left. But there's no clock, no calendar to help me.

It's still light, so that's something.

Nobody's here—no sign of Pearl or Zeke Turner's guards. I touch my face. The scratches are back. So are the bruises on my arms and legs. There's a ruckus outside. I hear men, shouting.

A horse neighs, terrified and angry.

It jolts every nerve in my body. I leap off the bed and zoom to the window. I try to yank it open, but it refuses to move. Frustrated, I lean my head against the glass. Below me, soldiers shove one another as they gather around a frantic bay mare. Nostrils flaring, she looks ready to explode. Her delicate ears curve inward, and her black tail almost reaches the ground. There's a perfect white star on her forehead.

Pandora?

A man with grizzled hair hangs onto her lead rope, and it's almost like watching a movie in slow motion. My brain is having a hard time keeping up with what's actually happening. Pandora breaks loose; Caroline screams at a soldier.

Gideon strides toward them.

But Caroline ignores him. She gathers up her skirts and races after Pandora. That lead rope snaps around the mare's slender legs like a bullwhip.

She could fall at any minute.

I'm about to abandon the window when another man steps into view. His slouch hat sports a feather, and there are enough gold buttons on his dark blue jacket to make an admiral jealous. With a sword at his side, he marches toward the soldiers. They turn and salute.

Is this Gideon's major?

It takes less than a minute to slip into my disguise. I pull on the skirt and peasant blouse, then bind my head in a turban. What about shoes? I'll need to run, and run fast, so I shove my feet into a pair of Caroline's boots.

The back stairs are in exactly the same place—just as dark and just as narrow. Gripping the handrail with one hand and my iPhone with the other, I creep down. A couple of steps creak and I freeze, waiting for someone to grab me.

But nobody does.

At the bottom, there's a door that opens into the kitchen. Two women bend over a hearth glowing with hot coals; another holds a little girl who reminds me of Hope. Putting a finger to my lips, I shake my head.

They understand.

There's a knot of soldiers near the barn. I slide past them, invisible as a ghost. In Caroline's world, nobody pays attention to black people. Our unseen hands get the work done; our faces blend into the background like beetles on a dirt floor. Someone races up behind me. Skidding to a halt, I turn around.

Gideon gulps. "You're back?"

"For a little while," I say. "What day is it?"

"Friday," he says, rolling his eyes as if I've just asked a really dumb question. "July seventeenth."

"Phew." This means I'm still in plenty of time. "I have something to tell the major—about tomorrow's battle."

"At Fort Wagner?"

"Yes."

"How do you know about that?" Gideon says.

I hold up my iPhone. "Where's the major?"

"With Caroline," he says. "And she's in trouble."

From around the corner, comes a commanding voice. I'm about to step forward when the major's puppy scampers up. With an excited yelp, Lobo twists and twirls around my ankles like a Furby on overdrive. I scoop him into my arms. Three more strides and I'm in full view of Caroline and—

"Major Van Houten," Gideon whispers in my ear.

I whisper back. "Is he Dutch?"

"I think so."

Of course he is, because who else but a Dutchman would have a keeshond puppy in Mississippi when everyone else owns hound dogs? The major's back is toward me. He nods at Caroline, then jerks his head toward Pearl.

"Is this the missing girl?"

"No major," I say. "That would be me."

He whirls around. "Who are you?"

With my scratched-up face and bruised arms, I must look like something the cat dragged in—or a slave who's been beaten. The last thing he'll expect is me, introducing myself in Dutch.

"Ik ben Samantha DeVries."

Major Van Houten's eyes open wide. His blond eyebrows almost shoot off the top of his freckled forehead.

"Ik hou van je hond," I say, telling the astonished major that I really like his dog. As if he understands, Lobo licks my face. When I get home, I'm going to beg Mom and Dad for another puppy, just like the major's.

He says, "You speak Dutch?"

"Yes."

"Why"

"Because my father's from Holland."

Not exactly true, but close enough. It takes the major a few seconds to process this. A black girl who speaks his language?

But not very well.

I only have a few words of Dutch, and I think I've used them all up. If Major Van Houten gets into a serious conversation, I will be lost.

With no trace of an accent, he says, "You have blue eyes."

"So do you."

For a moment, we stare at one another. He doesn't blink, and neither do I. Maybe I should tell the major about my mother's doctoral thesis on black people with blue eyes. I bet that would really get his attention.

Gideon steps forward. "Major, I believe Samantha has something important to tell you—about the battle tomorrow. Shall we go to your office?"

The major blinks.

I win.

"Very well," he says, still staring at me.

I guess my Dutch words and blue eyes have intrigued him. For now, anyway.

I hand the major his dog. "Cute puppy."

"Thank you." He glances at Caroline. "You're in big trouble, but I'll deal with it later."

Caroline tosses her head, then pushes past the major. "You came back," she says, pulling me into a hug. "Why?"

"I'll deal with it later," I whisper.

"Like the major?" she replies, and I have a hard time keeping a straight face.

❧ 36 ❧

CAROLINE

Mississippi, July 1863

WE STEP FROM BLISTERING HEAT into the coolness of my house and Sam says that she's going to make a deal with the major.

"Good luck," I say. "I doubt he's a gambling man."

Not like my father who'd wager a bet on anything that moved, including a pair of box turtles he and Mr. Hamilton used to race on our front porch. I've left Pandora in the barn with Pearl and Oscar standing guard. The major promised no harm would come to her, at least, not right now.

There's no time for Sam and me to talk.

We follow the major into Mama's parlor. He sits behind my mother's table while Gideon pulls out her velvet chairs. Waving him off, Sam pins her eyes on the major. They're even bluer than his.

She says, "I'll make you a deal."

"That's very generous of you," Major Van Houten says, voice dripping with sarcasm. "What kind of a deal would you have in mind?"

"If you guarantee Caroline and Pandora safe passage to New Orleans, I will tell you—"

The major laughs. "What, exactly?"

"About Fort Wagner," Sam says.

He takes a quick breath, then glares at Gideon. "That was classified information, Lieutenant."

"I didn't tell her, sir."

"Me neither," I say.

But I can guess how Sam found out. She searched that mysterious place she calls the *Internet*. One day I'd like to go there. I shall ask Sam to come back and get me as soon as this horrible war is over. Just for a visit, of course. I couldn't leave my horse and my family forever.

"So," Sam says. "Are we on, Major?"

"On what?"

"The same page," I blurt out.

He frowns at me. "What do you mean?"

There's no point in trying to explain Sam's words to a man who's firmly stuck in the nineteenth century. He won't understand, and even if he does, he'll never admit it.

Sam leans across Mama's table. "Do we have a deal or not?"

"I don't make deals with"—the major looks down his beaky nose—"servants."

Gideon coughs. "You might want to this time."

"What do *you* know about it?"

"Hear her out," Gideon says. "Sir."

I shoot him a grateful look because I know he's taking a risk by challenging the major. Gideon has no idea what Sam's about to say. Neither do I, but I know it will be powerful.

The major sighs. "Very well."

"I'm from the future," Sam says, as cool and calm as the inside of a watermelon. "I can tell you about many amazing things that are going to happen." She pauses. "Long after you're dead, there will be two world wars, men will fly to the moon, and a black man will be elected president."

He flinches. "Oh, really?"

"Yes, really," Sam says.

The major raises one eyebrow. "Prove it."

Slowly, Sam pulls out her iPhone and lays it on Mama's table. The screen shows Barack Obama being sworn in, followed by a parade down Pennsylvania Avenue. Flags wave and bands play; soldiers salute their new commander in chief.

Major Van Houten can't take his eyes off it.

Then the screen flips to fat little birds that get fired from slingshots. The evil pig's house blows up. Firing again, the birds destroy a wooden tower. The major's mouth drops open.

"What *is* this?"

"*Angry Birds*," I say. Sam and I have been playing this game for a week. My score is better than hers.

She grins. "It's an iPhone."

Fear, curiosity, and disbelief flash across the major's face. He turns pink, then deathly white as he grips the arms of his chair like he's about to pass out. If he does, I'll have to find Mama's smelling salts. I'm sure there's a jar around here somewhere. Biting back a smile, I glance at Gideon.

He lets out his breath. "Is *this* what you were talking about?"

"Amazing, isn't it?"

"Yes."

At a loss for words, the major reaches for Sam's phone but pulls back as if afraid it will bite him. Sam taps the screen and switches games.

Now it's chess—with zombies and vampires.

Another tap, and up comes my favorite video of One Direction. Music fills Mama's stuffy parlor like it's never been filled before. Snapping my fingers, I bop to the beat of "One Way or Another." Gideon taps his foot.

The music stops.

With a flourish, Sam aims her iPhone at the major. He just sits there, eyes practically bugging out of his head. Then Sam whirls around and snaps a photo of Gideon and me. I hope we don't look as silly as Major Van Houten.

He gasps for air like a hooked fish.

Sam steps around his desk and shows him the photos. He blinks and shakes his head. Maybe he's not happy with the one she took of him. As her fingers tap the screen, the major's face turns paler and paler. He looks more shocked than Mama did when Pandora dumped me in the duck pond.

"Enough," he chokes out.

I know exactly how he feels. It took me a week to absorb a tiny piece of what Sam shared with me. The major has had less than five minutes. Sam clicks off her iPhone and slips it into her pocket.

She says, "Do you have telegraph?"

"Yes, yes, of course we do," the major says. "It's at our headquarters in Vicksburg."

Sam nods. "How long does it take for a telegram to get from Washington to here?"

Gideon says, "A day, sometimes less."

"Unless the Rebels have cut our lines," the major says. "Why do you ask?"

"Because I will tell you right now what happens at Fort Wagner, but you're not going to believe me until you get confirmation from Washington," Sam says. "So that will mean Sunday, right?"

"Or Monday," Gideon says.

The major picks up Papa's pen and twirls it around his fingers. Eyes narrowed, he looks directly at Sam. "So, let me get this straight," he says. "You want me to provide Miss Chandler with an armed escort to New Orleans, and in return you're going to tell me what happens at Fort Wagner tomorrow night?"

"Exactly," Sam says.

And I know exactly what she's doing. She's trying to prove that she has magic powers, that she can predict the future. I hold my breath, waiting for the major's response. He straightens his shoulders. Now that Sam's iPhone is out of sight, he's probably persuaded himself it was all a mirage.

"Do I have your word?" Sam says.

The major gives another sigh. "For now," he says. "But I'm not convinced."

"You will be," Sam says.

"Why?"

"Because on Sunday I will show you what happened at Fort Wagner."

"Show me?"

"Yes, Major," Sam says. "I will *show* you."

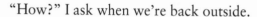

"How?" I ask when we're back outside.

We've left Gideon and the major in my mother's parlor, trying to cope with what Sam told them—the North loses at Fort Wagner, Colonel Shaw is killed. Gideon seems willing to believe it, but the major doesn't. He was so distracted that he didn't even object when I told him I was going to the barn.

Sam says, "Think about music videos."

"Okay."

"Well, I've got some of the battle at Fort Wagner."

"But that's impossible," I say. "Video wasn't invented until the nineteen fifties." It's a wild guess, but I'm probably not far off, given all I've learned in the past week. There are times when I wonder what century I'm living in—mine or Sam's.

She says, "This is like a play, with actors, but it's not on a stage. It's—"

From out of nowhere, someone slams into her.

37

SAMANTHA

Mississippi, July 1863

IT'S LIKE BEING GRABBED by a bully at school. "Got you this time," snarls a familiar voice.

"Help!" Caroline yells.

But I don't need it. In judo, this is called a "rear seizure" and Dad's taught me how to block it. Raising my shoulders, I jerk up my arms and stomp down hard on Zeke Turner's foot.

With a yelp, he lets go. "Oowwee!"

But I'm not done with him yet. Swinging to my right, I grab Zeke Turner's bony wrist, yank it up behind his back, and force him onto the ground. He struggles, so I twist his arm again.

He whimpers, just like Mr. Kelley did.

"Are you all right?" Caroline says, crouching beside me. Zeke Turner snatches at her skirt. I pinch his fingers, and he lets go, whimpering even louder.

"I'm fine," I say. "But get the major."

With luck, he'll arrest Zeke Turner and throw him in jail, or whatever it is they call it around here. Then again, they'll probably give him a warning and let him off. I'll have to be on guard.

Footsteps clatter down the front stairs.

The major hesitates, as if unsure what to do. "I saw what happened," he says, shaking his head. "But I don't believe it."

"Believe it, Major," Caroline says.

Carefully, I release Zeke Turner. He doesn't move. He's sprawled out like an ugly rag doll that nobody wants.

Gideon races up. "Is he dead?"

"No, he's a little tired."

"And scared," Caroline adds.

We've attracted another crowd. The same soldiers who clustered around Caroline's horse are now clustering around us, pointing at me as if I'm some sort of freak. The major orders his sergeant to take Zeke Turner into custody.

"Lock him up, and I'll deal with him later," he says.

I nudge Caroline. "Like he'll deal with you?"

She gives a nervous giggle, but the major doesn't hear, or chooses not to. His men drag Zeke Turner away. Feebly, he tries to resist, but it looks as if all the fight's gone out of him.

For now, anyway.

———∞———

Pearl is feeding Pandora an apple when we reach the barn. I stroke the mare's velvety nose and get slobber down the front of my blouse.

"You're worse than Nugget," I say.

She even looks like him, well, except for the color. Or maybe I'm fooling myself. Later, I'll show Caroline his pedigree. I haven't told her yet that our horses are related.

Proudly, Caroline introduces me to Raven and Meteor. "I'm taking them with me to New Orleans," she says, then looks at Pearl. "And you, too—if you'd like to come."

Pearl smiles. "Thank you."

"And tomorrow we shall all go riding," Caroline says.

"Sounds great," I say, "if the major will allow it."

But to my surprise, he makes no objection. He orders Gideon to accompany us, then invites Caroline and me to dinner—in the dining room with his officers.

"That'll be a first," Caroline says when we're up in her room. She's hunting through her armoire, choosing dresses for us to wear.

"What will?"

"A black girl at Mama's dining room table." She lays a pale green gown on the bed. It has a white collar and white undersleeves and tiny black buttons up the front. There's a black bow at the back. "This would look great on you."

Eyeing the full skirt, I say, "Will I have to wear a crinoline?"

"And a corset," Caroline says, grinning.

"Never."

"Come on," she says. "I'll wear one, too."

There's no arguing with her. She also insists on doing fancy stuff to my hair, and by the time she's finished, I hardly recognize myself. Mom wouldn't either. I've got ringlets and curls piled on top of my head like Scarlett O'Hara. As a finishing touch, Caroline ties a green ribbon in my hair and gives me a matching fan.

"Okay, your turn," I say, snatching up the flowery hat she wore in her portrait. "Put this on."

"No," she says. "I hate that silly hat."

I hold up my iPhone. "Just for a photo."

With a frown, she plunks it on her head. Crooked, just like it is in the portrait, and I manage to get off two shots before she rips it off again. "Thanks."

Then I remember her gifts.

She hugs the tube of shampoo and squeals with delight over the sports bra. "It's so comfortable," she says, twirling in front of her mirror. "I'll never take it off."

Giggling, we drench ourselves with Great Aunt Maude's perfume and slide our feet into silk slippers.

I pull Nugget's pedigree from my knapsack.

"Another surprise?" Caroline says.

I nod. "Our horses are related."

Her eyes open wide. "You have *got* to be kidding," she says, and I grin because she's sounding more and more like me every day. Pretty soon, she'll turn into a modern teenager.

"Look." I run my finger down the list.

"*Pandora?*" she says. "But she's never had a foal."

"Yet," I say.

The word hangs between us like a promise. Caroline

frowns, and I can almost see the wheels turning inside her head, the way they do in mine. Pandora has survived, but is it because of me?

"Does this mean what I think it means?" she says.

"Yes," I say. "Pandora will be okay."

Still frowning, Caroline says, "Is this why you came back, to save my horse so that Nugget would—?" Her voice trails off.

I'm tempted to lie, but she'd see right through it. "Yes."

For a moment, Caroline just stands there—every inch the Southern belle in her mother's favorite white gown. She plucks at a pink rosebud, then says, "I'd have done exactly the same thing."

I let out my breath. "Thank you."

We count the generations again and get totally lost trying to figure out how many great-grandparents separate Pandora from Nugget.

"She's his great-great-great- . . ." Caroline says, running her finger down the list again.

"Stop. My head's hurting already."

There's a soft tap on the door. Gideon says, "Are you ladies ready?"

"How do I look?" Caroline says, sounding anxious.

I think she likes him. "Fantabulous."

Dinner is formal and takes forever. The major and his officers wear long jackets with gold fringe on their shoulders; they know which knives and forks to use. Amid polite conversation, food is served that I've never eaten before—oysters, stuffed pheasant, and a syllabub that's so sweet it shocks my teeth. I'm about to ask for seconds when Caroline nudges me.

"Don't," she whispers.

"Why not?"

"Young ladies don't eat dessert."

I bite my lip. So does Caroline. For now, we're on our best behavior. I can hardly breathe. One more mouthful, and the laces on my corset will snap like frayed elastic.

Mom would have a lot to say about this.

But I think it's okay—for one night. It shows me another side of life and tells me that I have it pretty good in my world. I never realized that before. I took it all for granted.

The major wipes his mouth with a napkin and stands up. "I bid you all good night," he says, giving Caroline and me a stiff little bow. "Now, please excuse me."

The other officers, except for Gideon, excuse themselves as well, and now it's just me, Caroline, and the lieutenant. It's obvious they like one another. He can't take his eyes off her.

Well, duh-uh.

This is the first time Gideon's seen Caroline clean and dressed up. That gown isn't something I'd wear, but it looks pretty awesome on her.

"I'm kinda hot," I say, fanning myself.

"It's cooler on the porch," Caroline says.

I can take a hint. "See you guys later."

My crinoline's so wide that I almost get stuck in the door-way, but Caroline doesn't even notice. She's too busy staring at Gideon from across the table.

38

CAROLINE

Mississippi, July 1863

BEING ALONE WITH GIDEON inside the house is a whole lot different from being alone with him in the woods at midnight. I didn't feel awkward or shy out there, probably because I was scared to death.

Well, I'm even more scared now.

Gideon says, "May I come and sit beside you?"

"Yes." My voice is so quiet, I'm surprised he heard me.

He's halfway around the table when Beulah, my mother's maid, comes in. Arms folded, she stands in the corner and gives me the evil eye, just the way Mama would. Gideon falters. I place my hand on the chair beside me.

"Don't sit here," I say. "You'll crush my gown."

As if I cared about my silly dress.

To Beulah, I say, "I thought you'd left." I've not seen her since I got back.

She gives a curt nod. "The major's paying me to run the house," she says. "And it'll be here, in good order, when your Mama comes home. I ain't going no place."

"Thank you," I say. "I will tell Mama when I get down to New Orleans."

Now, please, will you leave us alone?

But Gideon smiles at her. "I'm from the North, ma'am, and I've never had food this good. Dinner was delicious, simply delicious, and you're a mighty fine cook."

"Why, thank you, sir," Beulah says.

She's not the cook, but I've never known Beulah to pass up a compliment.

"Might I ask a favor?" Gideon says.

She nods. "Be my pleasure."

"Then could I beg another small serving of that syllabub?" Gideon takes a step toward the door. "Just tell me where to go, and I shall fetch it myself."

"Oh, no, sir," she says. "I can't be allowing that. You just stay here, and I'll fetch it for you."

She gives me a frosty look that tells me I won't be getting any more syllabub. Mama has drilled Beulah well about young ladies and dessert. I couldn't eat it anyway. I'm too nervous.

And excited.

Gideon bows to Beulah, and she sweeps out, head up and even more regal than my mother. Years ago, I heard a rumor they were childhood playmates, just like Ruth and I were. But I didn't dare ask Mama about it. The door closes.

In a flash, Gideon is beside me. His eyelashes are even longer than mine. "How much time do we have?"

"About three minutes," I say.

He's going to kiss me, I know he is.

But he hesitates, looking so anxious, that I take matters into my own hands. I lean over and kiss his cheek. It's smooth and warm. He smells of fresh air and leather, and—

He sneezes.

"Oh, I'm so sorry," Gideon says, reaching for a napkin. He blushes pinker than the rosebuds on my dress. Then he sneezes again. It reminds me of Spinner, snorting at the rocks he pretended to be afraid of.

"What's wrong?" I say.

His blush deepens. "I think it's—"

"What?"

"Your perfume."

Oh, no!

My sister's bottle of *Camellia* that Sam and I threw about. I must smell like Papa's greenhouse.

"So, did he kiss you?" Sam says. We're back in my room, about to shed our crinolines and petticoats.

"No."

"Why not?"

"Because I kissed him first."

Sam gives me a high five. "Cool beans," she says. "Then what happened?"

"He sneezed."

Sam laughs so hard, she almost bursts out of her corset. Working fast, I unlace it.

"Why?" she says, breathless.

"This." I grab Louise's wretched perfume and throw it across the room. The heavy bottle bounces off my armoire and rolls beneath the bed.

"Next time, wear *eau de cheval*," Sam says.

"Is that Dutch?"

"No, it's French for 'horse water.'"

"Ugh," I say.

Sam grins. "Better than *eau de toilette*."

But it doesn't register until Sam tells me that *toilet* in her world means the place where you take care of personal business. It's also the name given to a diluted perfume.

"How do you know this?" I ask.

"Chemistry class at school," she says, pulling on her tank top. "We had to research the history of perfume. Toilet water goes all the way back to Cleopatra. Queen Wilhelmina of The Netherlands used to bathe in it."

"Sounds awful," I say.

"Yeah," Sam agrees. "The boys hated it. They wanted to make stink bombs, not perfume."

"Do you have a beau?"

Sam pulls the ribbon from her hair. "Like this?"

"Not a *bow*, silly. A *beau*, a young man you like." If she does, she's never talked about him.

She shrugs. "Kind of, but he doesn't know I exist."

"Why?"

"Because he's a senior, and I'm—"

"So, how old is that?" I can't even imagine what school must be like. My sister attended the Rosewood Seminary for Young Ladies in Natchez, but Mama wouldn't let me go. I don't think she trusted me to keep out of trouble.

"Eighteen."

"Does he ride?"

"Yeah," she says. "A snowboard."

"Is that a new breed?" I say.

She's told me all about Thoroughbreds, Quarter Horses, and Appaloosas. She's explained that Dutch Warmbloods are fairly recent, but that Morgan horses go way back to the late 1700s. Sam pulls out her iPhone, clicks a few times, then hands it to me.

"That's a snowboard."

A boy with flying red hair hangs upside down, a piece of brightly painted wood strapped to his feet. I get dizzy just looking at him. The snow is blindingly white; the sky is bluer than I've ever seen.

"Is this him?" I ask.

"No, that's an Olympic dude."

"*Olympic?*"

"I'll explain tomorrow," she says, yawning.

We settle into bed. Lying beside Sam is like having a comfort cushion. Moonlight streams through my window, and I wonder if Gideon is thinking about me.

He's waiting at the barn when we get there at nine o'clock on Saturday morning. Oscar and Pearl have already fed and groomed the horses. I just have to choose which ones we're going to ride. I'll take Pandora, Pearl can have Allegra, and—

Gideon smiles at me.

I feel myself blush.

With a grin, Sam disappears into the tack room and comes out with my side saddle. "I'm gonna try this," she says. "Is that okay?"

"Yes," I say. "But we're going to race."

"Where?"

"Papa's racetrack."

39

SAMANTHA

Mississippi, July 1863

I'VE SEEN OLD PHOTOS of women jumping five-foot fences with side saddles, but I've never ridden in one before. It looks comfortable and scary, all at once. Oscar leads Meteor into the aisle. He glances at Caroline.

"This one for Miss Samantha?" he says.

Caroline nods, so Oscar hoists her awkward saddle onto Meteor's back, tightens the girth, and helps me to get on board. It's completely different from anything I've done before—both legs on the left side of a horse. But at least I'm wearing my breeches—not one of those cumbersome riding habits with a split skirt.

Gideon's already outside with Raven.

Pearl and Caroline ride out of the barn on their mares. I

follow with Meteor. He jiggles sideways, but without my legs wrapped around him, it's hard to keep him going straight. Oscar hands me a whip.

"Use this," he says, "in your right hand."

"I don't like whips."

"Neither do I," says the black man. "But you won't need to use it because this horse will know it's there and he'll respect it."

His words poke holes in my brain all the way to Mr. Chandler's half-mile racetrack. We pass empty cotton fields and a sloping meadow filled with rows of white army tents. Smoke curls upward from campfires; horses stand idle while attached to the shafts of chuck wagons. The grass is trampled flat.

Battle-weary soldiers lounge about. A few of them wave, and I can't help thinking about those brave men who're going to storm Fort Wagner tonight and die by the hundreds.

There's nothing I can do to stop it.

And if I tried, it would mess up the future.

Will I mess up Pandora's chances of survival? No, because the proof lies in Nugget's pedigree. But that could easily fall apart unless I intervene or someone else does.

It's kind of like the butterfly effect—a Monarch flutters its delicate wings above a remote pond in South America and causes a tsunami of epic proportions in Japan three weeks later. My brother, who's majoring in physics, says the idea is based on chaos theory.

He lost me right there.

All I know is, I can't stand back and do nothing. Also, I want to prove where I've been. I give Caroline the iPhone and she snaps a photo of me. Nobody will believe I'm riding side saddle. Correction—they're not going to believe *anything*. Well, except for Erik.

Maybe.

We race the horses. Meteor would've won if I hadn't been struggling with Caroline's saddle. I'm totally in awe of women who can ride in them, especially over fences. In the end, it's down to Gideon on Raven and Caroline on Pandora. They zoom around her father's track, neck and neck, but Pandora beats Raven by a nose.

Caroline pumps the air with her fist.

That's something else I've taught her. I'm going to miss her like crazy, and I wish I didn't have to leave, but—

The major rides by with two officers.

Is he checking up on Caroline—making sure she hasn't made a mad dash for New Orleans? But that's insane. Why would he waste his time on this when he's got battles to win?

Major Van Houten's an odd duck.

Then again, so are lots of Dutchmen, including my father. If he were here right now, he'd be telling Gideon to keep his heels down and Caroline to sit up straighter, never mind they're in the midst of a horrible war. As for me? Well, he'd be so shocked to see me riding side saddle, he might actually be speechless.

For once.

We take a different trail home and ride past a large pond with a very small beach. Frogs sit on lily pads among pink and white blossoms; dragonflies skim the surface. And who knows what's hiding amid the tangled roots of tupelo trees that rise from the banks like monsters from one of my brother's fantasy novels.

I am ready to melt. "Let's go for a swim."

"Here?" Caroline says.

"Why not?"

Somehow, I manage to dismount without stabbing myself on the pommels. I pull off my boots, remove Caroline's side saddle, and remember—at the last minute—to empty my pockets. I give my iPhone and earbuds to Pearl, then I vault back onto Meteor. He needs no urging. Within minutes we're in the water up to his belly. He starts to splash.

Behind me, Caroline says, "Watch out for the snappers."

"Snappers?"

"Turtles," she says, grinning. "And alligators."

I hope she's kidding.

Pearl stays near the edge with Allegra, but Gideon rides Raven in to join us. It's like being with my friends at the beach in Connecticut. I tell them about the lottery that Jenna and I won.

"Will you wear"—Caroline blushes and glances at Gideon—"one of those, um, bathing suits?"

"Yes," I say, wishing I had one now.

But hey, wait a minute. I'm wearing a sports bra. That covers me far more than a bikini does. So I pull off my shirt, tell an astonished Caroline to hold Meteor's reins, and leap off his back. Gideon turns the other way.

"It's okay," I yell, treading water. "You can look."

Next thing I know, Caroline's up to her shoulders in the water, kissing Pandora on the nose. Stupidly, I reach into my pocket for my iPhone because this would be *the* perfect picture, but, of course, Pearl has it. I glance toward her. As usual she's way ahead of me.

Ahead of *everyone*.

With her arm looped through Allegra's reins, Pearl aims my iPhone at us—at me, at Caroline, and at Gideon, who's still not sure whether to take the plunge and join the fun. But Raven has other ideas. Snorting and backing up, he's still a bit wary of all this water.

Stallions can be such wimps.

I scramble onto Meteor's slippery back and take him swimming. I've never swum with a horse before, and all I can think about is doing this with Nugget next Sunday. He'll probably snort at the waves and jump over them. I will probably fall off.

Jenna will laugh.

Is she going to believe all this—even with the photos I've taken and me swearing the truth on a stack of *Dressage Today* magazines? Erik might, but only because he's a time travel geek and he wants to believe in it, badly.

40

CAROLINE

Mississippi, July 1863

GIDEON IS STANDING WITH RAVEN in the shallow
water when Sam and I finally drag ourselves onto the beach.
Pond weed sticks to my face; my blouse is plastered to my
skin. Horrified, I look down. Gideon takes off his jacket.

"Put this on."

From a nearby lily pad he plucks a blossom that's about
to open, then bows and gives it to me. The petals are white,
tinged with pink, and so utterly perfect that I burst into tears.

"You're getting all wet," Sam says.

Laughing through my tears, I slip into Gideon's jacket and
ask Sam if she'd like to ride Pandora back to the barn.

"You mean it?" she says. "Like, will she—?"

"Let's try."

"Okay, but why?"

"Because I want you to ride my horse before, you know—before you . . ."

I hold Pandora's head while Sam saddles her up. Not the side saddle because Sam will need both legs around Pandora if she decides to act up.

But she doesn't.

She behaves just like Spinner did, and I'm guessing that Sam's working her magic again. Pandora arches her neck and dances a little. Her ears swivel back and forth. She looks as if she's ready for anything, including Major Van Houten, who's trotting toward us and looking quite thunderous.

He glares at Gideon. "You're not dressed appropriately, Lieutenant. Put your jacket back on immediately."

"It's my fault, Major," I say. "I fell off my horse. Lieutenant Palmer was kind enough to—"

The major arches one eyebrow. "We haven't had rain for a week, and I don't see any puddles," he says. "So how did you get wet?"

Beside me, Sam gives a muffled snort.

"Miss Chandler's horse bolted into the pond with her," Gideon says. How he's keeping a straight face, I have no idea. Sam turns the other way. Her shoulders are shaking. Pearl, as usual, remains inscrutable.

"And I suppose you rode in to rescue her?"

"Yes, sir."

"Very well," the major says, clearly outgunned. "Report to me when you get back. That will be all." He wheels his gray gelding around, and the other two officers fall into place behind him. The moment they're out of earshot, we collapse laughing. Even Gideon.

"You are so *not* a good soldier," Sam says.

He tries to look chagrined but fails, and I wonder what he did before joining the army. Maybe he was a student at a college up north, like Harvard or Yale. That's where Theo wanted to go before this horrible war got in the way.

Will it ever be over?

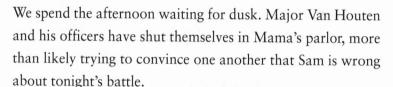

We spend the afternoon waiting for dusk. Major Van Houten and his officers have shut themselves in Mama's parlor, more than likely trying to convince one another that Sam is wrong about tonight's battle.

She's unusually quiet as she helps me pack boxes and trunks to take down to New Orleans. They will go on the buckboard that I'm going to insist the major give me, along with an escort. From Louise's armoire I scoop up the dresses and bonnets she left behind, including her wedding gown. But who knows if she'll get to wear it. Her betrothed is with General Bragg's army, somewhere in Georgia.

After reclaiming Mama's teacups from the major, I wrap them in newspaper and place them carefully in a wooden crate filled with straw. Then I ransack Papa's library for the books I know he'd like to have.

What shall I take for Theo?

"How about this?" Sam says, holding out his buckskin vest.

I'm surprised he left it behind. "Perfect."

We are not invited to join the major and his officers for dinner, so Sam and I head downstairs to the kitchen. The cook tells us to help ourselves, but I cannot taste a thing. I don't think Sam can, either. I ask if I can watch the film that she will show the major tomorrow, but Sam shakes her head.

"It'll run the battery down."

The news finally comes on Sunday afternoon. We're in my bedroom when a dusty soldier riding a sweaty bay gallops up. The horse has barely stopped when the man leaps off, pulls something from his saddlebag, and races into the house.

Ten minutes later, there's a knock on my door.

Gideon says, "The major would like to see you."

"Both of us?" I say.

There's a hesitation. "Yes."

"Zero hour," Sam says, picking up her iPhone. "Let's go."

Gideon waits at the top of the stairs, and we follow him down in a somber procession. Is it my imagination or has the house gone into mourning? There's hardly any sound, no soldiers bustling about. The chair behind Mama's bombé chest is empty. Her parlor drapes are closed. It's like a tomb in here.

The major is alone.

In the half light, his hair looks more gray than blond, the lines on his face are deeper than they were yesterday. "There are only two outcomes in a battle," he says. "You win or you lose . . . and we lost."

"I'm sorry," Sam says.

There's a catch in her voice, and though we haven't talked

about it, I know she's feeling this more than any of us. Those were black soldiers who lost their lives last night.

"So," the major goes on, "you had a fifty percent chance of being correct with your prediction."

She nods. "Yes."

"But this doesn't mean I'm willing to believe—"

Sam pulls out her iPhone and lays it beside a stack of papers on the major's desk. "We made a deal on Friday. You agreed to guarantee safe passage for Caroline and her horses to New Orleans in return for me showing you what actually happened at Fort Wagner."

"Yes, well—"

"Write it down," Sam says.

"You won't take my word?"

Sam hands him a blank page torn from my diary. "Caroline will take four horses of her choosing," she says, sounding like Papa's lawyer. "You will supply a buckboard, a driver, and six soldiers to escort her to her aunt's house in New Orleans."

"Shall I write it in blood?"

"Ink will do fine."

The major reaches for Papa's pen. The sound of it scratching across the paper is all I can hear. The noise from outside— men talking, carts rumbling by—fades into the background.

"Seal it," Sam says.

With a sigh, the major folds the paper, drips a puddle of red wax on it, and presses down hard with a heavy brass stamp. He hands the document to me.

"Satisfied?" he says.

I nod. "Perfectly. I shall leave tomorrow morning."

"As you wish."

He tells Gideon to lock Mama's door so nobody can interrupt him, Gideon, Sam, and me. I guess the major doesn't want his other officers to see what Sam's about to show us.

☙ 41 ❧

SAMANTHA

Mississippi, July 1863

TRYING TO EXPLAIN FILM TO GIDEON and the
major is like explaining quantum physics to a toddler—not
that I know anything about physics, quantum or otherwise.
That's Erik's department, not mine.

"This isn't the *real* battle," I say. "It's a play based on
what actually happened. But the actors aren't on a stage,
they're—

"In a movie," Caroline says.

"It'll be obvious when you see it," I add.

The major looks more skeptical than ever. Gideon just
shakes his head, then arranges chairs by the major's desk so
we can all see what's happening on my iPhone's tiny screen.
The first few minutes are brutal, so I warn Caroline to close
her eyes.

Gideon and the major flinch.

As the movie unfolds, I try to imagine how they must feel, watching a battle that happened yesterday on a gadget that won't be invented for another hundred forty-five years. On top of that, they won't be able to tell anyone else because nobody will believe them. And if they try, they'll be branded as whackos.

The final scene is a tearjerker, with men dying left and right until, finally, Colonel Robert Gould Shaw is killed. I hear a muffled sob and glance at the major. He's wiping his eyes.

Gideon sniffs. "That was amazing."

"So sad," Caroline says.

Major Van Houten finally asks the question I've been waiting for him to ask. "Who wins?"

"You do, Major."

"When?"

"Eighteen sixty-five." I can't remember the exact date of Appomattox when General Lee surrendered, even though Mom has tried to drum it into my thick head, along with everything else about this awful war.

"Two more years?" the major says. "Can't you—?"

"No," I say, as gently as possible. "I can't change history." Bad enough I've meddled with Caroline and Pandora— I just have to hope it was the right thing to do.

I guess I'll find out when I get home.

An hour later, I stand in the driveway with Caroline and watch Gideon supervise the soldiers who're packing her small buckboard. Trunks and boxes pile up. A corporal almost drops Mama Chandler's crate of teacups and gets reamed out by Caroline. She will ride Pandora, with Pearl riding Meteor and Allegra pulling the buckboard.

Lieutenant Palmer is to ride Raven.

Much to Caroline's delight, the major has transferred Gideon to the Union headquarters in New Orleans, which is all of five miles from Aunt Maude's house. Who knew Major Van Houten had a touch of romance in his soul?

It's time for me to leave.

I don't want to be standing here at dawn tomorrow, waving them off, and then climbing up to Caroline's bedroom, in tears and alone. She has Gideon and Pearl—and she has her horse.

And now I need mine.

Quietly, I slip away and climb the stairs to Caroline's bedroom. I gather up my iPhone and my earbuds; I put on my *Barn Bratz* tank top. But before I have a chance to pull the dime from my knapsack, Caroline is there. So is Pearl.

"Don't go," Caroline says.

Pearl looks at me. "You must."

She understands, even though she knows less about me than Caroline does. But she's watched this happen before, so I guess it's not quite so scary for her. Caroline sits on the bed, and we wrap our arms around each other. How do you say good-bye to a girl from another century who's become your best friend in less than ten days?

"I'll miss you," I say.

"Me, too," Caroline says, hugging me hard enough to crack my ribs. "Write to me."

If only I could, but how do you get a letter from my world to hers? The Internet is great, but it hasn't figured out time travel yet. Neither has the post office, unless you count all those letters to Santa Claus that it delivers to the North Pole. Slowly, Caroline unsnaps her locket.

"Take this," she says, pressing it into my hand.

I push it away. "No, it's too precious."

"That's why I want you to have it."

"But I have nothing to give you," I say.

With a grin, Caroline plucks at her bra strap. "You already have."

If this were a commercial, we'd have models in lacy underwear and high heels strutting across the screen. They'd glance back over their shoulders and shoot pouty looks at the camera. Music would blast our eardrums, but all I hear are Caroline's sobs that she's trying hard to muffle.

Mom always said, *Don't prolong the agony.*

Rip it off fast like you're ripping off a Band-Aid. So I fish out my dime, hold onto it hard, and hope it takes me back to the place where I need to go.

The walls are plain white, the alarm clock says three-thirty, and that window fan chugs along like the little train that could. With a sigh of relief, I stagger to the window. Dad's still out there with Hughie-Dewey. It's like they're frozen in time.

This is totally nuts.

I've been gone over a week, but nothing here has moved forward. Yet in Caroline's time, it does. Even though I just left her a few minutes ago, it might be tomorrow morning by now. She could be on her way to New Orleans. Will she and Pandora be safe?

Will Nugget?

In a panic, I call Mom, hoping she's remembered to turn her cell phone on. It rings and rings and I'm about to hang up when she answers, sounding breathless.

"Is everything all right?" I blurt.

"Yes, I'm cleaning stalls."

"Where's Nugget?"

"In the paddock."

"Can you see him?"

"Not from here." There's a pause. "Sam, are you okay? You sound a bit—"

"Mom, just make sure he's okay, please."

I hear the sound of her footsteps and can imagine her striding down the barn's aisle, horses on both sides whickering and clattering buckets in the hopes of being fed. It's an hour later in Connecticut, so evening feed is fast approaching.

Mom says, "Sam, he's just fine."

"Really?"

"Would you like to speak with him?"

Now I feel stupid, but after the week I've just had, I'm not going to blame myself. "Just give him a kiss for me, okay? And tell him I love him to bits."

"I think he already knows," Mom says, and the noise of her kissing my horse comes through loud and clear. "There," she says. "Feel better now?"

"Yeah." I pause. "I have a lot to tell you."

She laughs. "You've only been gone a few hours. It must've been an exciting flight."

"It was," I say. "We had tornadoes."

And that's not all.

But I keep my mouth shut. I don't want to explain all this over the phone. I don't even know if I *can* explain it and if anyone will believe me.

Exhaustion overtakes me, and Mom has barely said goodbye when I fall into a dreamless sleep.

I am five minutes late getting downstairs for dinner, but at least I'm wearing my jeans skirt. After the clothes I wore at Caroline's, this is a breeze. I make polite conversation with Hughie-Dewey and his transparent wife and am secretly glad that Carrie didn't come home from play practice. She forgot I was coming and made plans with friends.

The rest of my weekend goes by in a blur.

I ride horses for Dad, swim laps in the enormous pool, and manage to corner Hughie-Dewey by himself to ask questions about the house. But he knows very little which is odd, given he's a Civil War buff. It seems he's only interested in the battles and bloodshed, so I guess all those portraits in the upstairs hall are just for show.

As we walk past them, I have a brilliant idea.

It's so brilliant, I almost choke. Trying to keep my hand steady, I point to Caroline's portrait. "I'd like to buy it."

I have a little money saved up, and this would prove beyond a shadow of a doubt where I've been. Mom and

Erik—and Dad—will have to believe me once they see my photo of Caroline, scowling beneath her flowery hat, lined up beside her portrait.

Hughie-Dewey takes it down.

"Here, you may have it. My wife has never liked this picture," he says. "Besides, with all the money your father's going to spend on my horses, the least I can do is give you a little gift."

––––––○○○○––––––

Mom meets us at the airport. Dad slings our bags into the trunk and climbs in beside her. I slouch in the back while he talks a mile a minute about our weekend. I've not said a word to Dad about my adventure because I want to tell Mom first. As we wait at a traffic light, she turns around.

"Sam, you're very quiet. Are you all right?"

"Yes. How's Nugget?"

"Exactly the same as the last time you asked."

Poor Mom. I pestered her all weekend with phone calls and texts. I guess I'm still not convinced that what I did was right. I'll probably always worry, now that I know how vulnerable horses were back then.

I'm worried about Caroline, too.

But when I think about it logically, she's been dead for a long time—at least in my world—and so is everyone else, including Pandora. But Nugget is here, so doesn't that prove Pandora survived? As Erik once said, there are no rules for time travel.

I'm having a hard time with this.

To me, Caroline is alive and well. She's filling my heart, and I wish she were here. We could have so much fun. I'd teach her about dressage and show jumping, and she'd get to meet Jenna and—

Mom's car stops abruptly.

Yanking open the door, I race into the barn. There's a tiny *Welcome Home* sign on Nugget's door. He looks over it, whickering. Mom has even left a bag of carrots in a bucket so I'd have a treat for him.

She thinks of everything—just like Pearl.

Dad and Erik have gone to bed by the time I sit down with Mom. We're in the family room, sprawled on the couch with mugs of hot cocoa, even though the heatwave I left on Friday still hasn't broken. It was cooler in Mississippi.

"Something's up," Mom says. "If you want to talk, I'm ready to listen."

"I don't know where to start."

"The beginning's always a good idea."

On the coffee table, I clear a space for my iPhone, the *Barn Bratz* tank top, Caroline's portrait, and her locket. The dime is tucked safely in my knapsack. I'm not sure about picking it up again—maybe with rubber gloves or something.

"Pretty girl," Mom says. "Who is it?"

So I start the story; and the further I get into it, the crazier it sounds. But Mom doesn't interrupt. She just sits and listens the way she always does, nodding occasionally and asking a quick question if something isn't clear.

I don't leave anything out.

And when I get to the part about Zeke Turner, Mom wraps me in a hug so fierce and strong it reminds me of the one Caroline gave me just before I left.

"But I took care of him, Mom."

She smiles. "I'm sure you did."

It takes longer than I expected. There's so much to tell. As I fill in the details, I show her the photos and videos I took, and not once does she purse her lips or make exasperated sounds. Mom believes me, right from the beginning, because she knows I would never make up something like this.

"Show me the dime," she says.

"Be careful."

Mom peers inside my knapsack, then carefully pulls the dime out with a paper towel. "Sweet," she says, turning it around. "Very collectible."

"And very scary," I add.

"What shall we do with it?"

I look at the wall where Mom's collection of coins hangs in special display boxes. The dime will be safe up there, encased in acrylic—far away from my iPhone and my tank top. I point and say, "That."

"Are you sure?"

"Yes."

There's a pause, then Mom says, "You could make a lot of money with this dime. Enough to pay for college."

"It would cause trouble."

"Yes," Mom says, nodding. "Lots of trouble."

"So let's leave it alone."

The implications overpower me. I can't think about them right now, and Mom knows this. She reaches for her iPad. "Let's find out what happened to Caroline and her family."

But do I want to?

"You must," Mom says, sounding exactly like Pearl. "Otherwise you'll always wonder. Pretend it's a research project for school."

So I give Mom all the names and we discover that Caroline Chandler married Gideon Palmer in 1867 and that they moved to Boston, where Gideon became a lawyer and fought for civil rights.

"What about the horses?" I daren't look.

Mom scrolls down the page. "It says here that they ran a successful breeding farm. They also had three children—two boys and a girl named Samantha."

So, of course, I burst into tears. "And when I have a kid," I say, wiping my nose, "I'll call it Caroline."

"Even if it's a boy?"

"Theo, then," I say. "What happened to him? Does it say?"

We search the site but find no mention. I hope Theo survived the war. Caroline was always so worried about him running away to join the army.

"Tell me more about Pearl," Mom says.

She's the hardest one to pin down. Describing Caroline and Gideon to Mom was easy—a tomboy and a dreamer—but Pearl is a challenge. "She was wicked smart," I finally say. "And she was always there when you needed her, even before you knew that you needed her"—I catch my breath—"kind of like you."

"Thanks." Mom twists her pearl ring.

It's been a part of her hand ever since I can remember, but I don't remember asking her about it before.

"Where did you get it?"

"From my mother," Mom says, "who got it from her mother, and so on. It's been in our family for many years. One day, it'll be yours." The gold is worn so thin on one side, it looks ready to break. "Did I ever tell you what pearl means?"

"No."

"It comes from a Greek word, *Margaron*."

"Like Margaret?"

"Yes," Mom says.

Margaret's my middle name—same as my grandmother. Mom's name is Gretchen, which she now reminds me is a derivative of Margaret, along with Margot and Marjorie and Margeurite. "Then there's Peg, Rita, and Daisy," Mom goes on. "They're all part of the Margaret family, and my ancestors have used all of them."

"Including Pearl?"

Startled, we look at one another.

Mom shakes her head. "No, it couldn't be, could it?"

"Why not?" I say.

Mom's genealogy is stuck in 1875. Maybe this will unstick it. "Pandora's first foal was called Black Pearl, so—" I scroll further down the page and find the name I'm looking for.

Pearl.

"Here she is," I say, shoving the iPad at Mom.

"Pearl Fremont," she reads out. "A free black girl from Illinois, briefly a slave in Mississippi during the Civil War, then personal assistant to Caroline and Gideon Palmer at their horse farm in Wakefield, Massachusetts." There's a pause. "Married Isaac Fremont of Boston in eighteen seventy-one; two daughters—Daisy and Faith."

"Daisy," I say. "That's your connection."

Mom gives me a fist bump. We both know it's a long shot . . . but Pearl, *my* Pearl, just might be related to my mother—and to me.

"Are you going to tell Jenna about this?" Mom says.

"Should I?"

"Only if you think she'll believe you."

With Mom's help, I tell Dad and Erik the next morning. Dad just keeps shaking his head, and it's obvious that he's having a hard time believing it. But my brother is madly jealous.

"I want that dime," he says.

Mom holds up her hand. "Off limits," she says. "Besides, it only works in special circumstances. So unless you're planning to borrow your sister's iPhone, wear her tank top, and stretch out on Caroline Chandler's four-poster bed in Mississippi while listening to Lady Gaga, it won't work."

Erik sighs. "Why does Sam get all the fun?"

"Mostly, it wasn't," I say, "especially the part about being a slave."

He goes kind of quiet after that, but on our way to the barn he tells me I did the right thing. "You probably saved Nugget's life."

✌ Epilogue ✌
SAMANTHA

Connecticut, present day

THE BEACH RIDE IS EVERY BIT as awesome as I predicted. Nugget jumps the waves, I fall off, and Jenna laughs.

She sounds just like Caroline.

So far I haven't told Jenna about my crazy adventure.

But I will tonight. We're having a sleepover at my house and we'll sit on the bed just like I did with Caroline, but with popcorn and cutoffs, not cornbread and bloomers.

And if I know Jenna, she'll be all over it.

About the Author

MAGGIE DANA'S FIRST RIDING LESSON, at the age of five, was less than wonderful. She hated it so much, she didn't try again for another three years. But all it took was the right horse and the right instructor and she was hooked.

After that, Maggie begged for her own pony and was lucky enough to get one. Smoky was a black New Forest pony who loved to eat vanilla pudding and drink tea, and he became her constant companion. Maggie even rode him to school one day and tethered him to the bicycle rack . . . but not for long because all the other kids wanted pony rides, much to their teachers' dismay.

Maggie and Smoky competed in Pony Club trials and won several ribbons. But mostly, they had fun—hanging out with other horse-crazy girls. At horse camp, Maggie and her teammates spent one night sleeping in the barn, except they didn't get much sleep because the horses snored. The next morning, everyone was tired and cranky, especially when told to jump without stirrups.

Born and raised in England, Maggie now makes her home on the Connecticut shoreline. When not mucking stalls or grooming shaggy ponies, Maggie enjoys spending time with her family and writing the next book in her TIMBER RIDGE RIDERS series.

TIMBER RIDGE RIDERS

WITH NINE EXCITING BOOKS—and more to come—this action-packed series has already captured over 350 glowing reviews. So grab your helmet and join the Timber Ridge girls as they ride into a stormy summer filled with secrets and lies and impossible dreams.

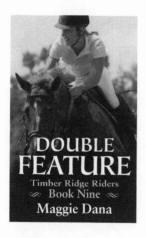

DOUBLE FEATURE ... book #9 in the Timber Ridge Riders series by Maggie Dana is now available in print from Amazon.com, your local bookstore, and in e-book from Amazon, B&N, Kobo, and Apple.

Visit the Timber Ridge web site for information about all the Timber Ridge books.

www.timberriddgeriders.com

To sign up for the Timber Ridge mailing list, send your email address to:
timberridgeriders@gmail.com

Note: all email addresses are kept strictly confidential.

Made in the USA
San Bernardino, CA
06 May 2014